PRAISE FOR THE

"Chaplinsky takes a famous physics paradox and brings it back down to earth, using it to rethink the ways in which families relate and interrelate and disintegrate. A collage that assembles itself into a sneaky whole in which it's not always easy to tell what the truth is."

—Brian Evenson, author of *Song For the Unraveling of the World*

"As confirmed by *The Paradox Twins*, Joshua Chaplinsky is one of a handful of American novelists creating the literature of the future: dazzling, original and subversive."

—Steve Erickson, author of *Zeroville* and *Shadowbahn*

"Like a coy, uncanny hybrid of J.G. Ballard and John Carpenter, the Oulipo and the Bizarro, *The Paradox Twins* is an engrossing and digressive trip through birth and back, stuffed from end to end with mystic weirdness and meta-gags with style to spare."

—Blake Butler, author of *Alice Knott* and *300,000,000*

"Family, like life (and fiction!), requires some assembly. And in the skewed, dark, strangely tender landscape of *The Paradox Twins*, all the pieces are placed in the reader's hands."

—Kathe Koja, author of *The Cipher*

"Every once in a while a shoebox novel has an understory. *The Paradox Twins* goes even deeper, is pretty much multiphasic — how much more meta can it get? Chaplinsky is here to show you."

—Stephen Graham Jones, author of *Mongrels* and *The Only Good Indians*

"A daring and inventive novel that does justice to the complicated nature of all stories, and all entanglements. Chaplinsky plays with form and structure like a pro, giving us a book that is many books—a haunting collage you might re-read the moment you've finished it."

—Lindsay Lerman, author of *I'm From Nowhere*

"A brain-bending epistolary work that defies genre, format and expectation, *The Paradox Twins* is part family drama, part sci-fi epic, part ghost story, and wholly original. Chaplinsky writes with bright, irreverent strangeness, but the most outlandish moments of this story never keep the reader at a distance or numb the emotional impact. We're right there with Max and Alan as they navigate the thorny mystery of their lives, their father's death, and their relationship to one another and to the world."

—Meredith Borders, *Fangoria*

"Imagine if you put *Rashomon*, Chuck Palahniuk, *House of Leaves*, Kubrick's *2001: A Space Odyssey* and the dysfunctional family dramedy of Wes Anderson into a blender. That's Joshua Chaplinsky's *The Paradox Twins*, a crackling new novel whose every twist and turn lands with emotionally-satisfying precision. Buy this book."

—Scott Wampler, *The Kingcast*

"A debut novel that discovers brand new territory and claims it as its own."

—Sadie Hartmann, aka Mother Horror

"...a stunningly complex and lovingly crafted book about the unfathomable mystery of family and how it evolves over time."

—Matt Hill, *Invert/Extant*

"Chaplinsky has annihilated the traditional novel narrative — never before have I had such a blast sifting through the rubble. Like an American Borges writing science fiction as directed by Wes Anderson. An achievement of challenging experiment with surprisingly mainstream appeal."

—Gabriel Hart, author of *A Return to Spring*

THE
PARADOX
TWINS

JOSHUA CHAPLINSKY

CL⊿SH

THE

PARADOX TWINS

JOSHUA CHAPLINSKY

CLASH

For my brothers

UNRAVELING THE PARADOX: A WEBMASTER'S INTRODUCTION

They say there are three sides to every story: yours, mine, and the truth. In the case of the so-called Paradox Twins, those three sides are represented by Max Langley's best-selling novel *Breakfast with the Monolith* (as well as the many drafts of its screenplay adaptation, currently mired in perpetual development hell), Albert Langley's infinitely more grounded memoir *The Paradox Twins*, and Millicent Blackford's own memoir, *The Third Twin*, which in my humble opinion is the least sensationalistic and most well written of the three.

But which of these accounts represents the actual truth? It depends on the day and who you ask. To quote legendary film producer Robert Evans's addendum to the three sides axiom: *...And no one is lying. Memories shared serve each differently.* In other words, truth is a rotating point of view. A constantly shifting coordinate on a flat circle, dependent on the observer. Or better yet, a combination of the concepts of eternal recurrence and quantum superposition, where the coordinate (POV) can be expressed as either True or False at any given time.

But in this day and age, we don't have to settle for a mere three points of view. The advent of the internet has given rise to an unlimited number of options where storytelling is concerned (and yes, a true story is still, inherently, a story), and everyone and their mother is invited to play in the sandbox. Don't like what an author did with your favorite character? Write some fan fiction. Don't like what George Lucas did with the Star Wars franchise? Re-edit his movies. Don't like the tracklist of the latest Kanye West album? That's why iTunes exists. Art is a living, breathing thing, affected by those around it. As I'm sure Paul Langley would agree, the mere observation of an object changes it. In physics this is called the Hawthorne Effect, but it applies to art as well. And yes, storytelling, even of the non-fiction variety, is an art.

And that's not even taking into account social media (and this is where things get dicey). When it comes to the pro-liferation of information, no entity muddies the waters more than Facebook or Twitter. The curation and aggregation of "facts" by the ignorant and uninformed creates an amor-phous narrative, one whose each and every iteration is her-alded as true. Snippets of headlines, memes, and shares are regurgitated without any fact-checking or quality control by acquaintances, friends of friends, or your great aunt Helene. Which is fine if the narrative you're participating in concerns the relationship status of a celebrity (because like rampaging advertising mascots, they cease to exist when we stop paying attention to them). It is, however, another thing entirely when it comes to scientific matters.

Don't consider misinformation a legitimate threat to empirical truth? Sure, it's funny when an aging pro athlete gets on national television and proclaims themselves a Flat-Earther, and we can all point and laugh and say, "Look at stupid!", but what about that popular actress-turned-mom who has her own website and some bold ideas about smallpox vaccinations? She's more than the punchline to a joke. And I'm not even going to touch on the gladiatorial arena that is modern day political discourse.

But I digress.

Now at this point you may find yourself wondering, if I deem myself such a champion of truth, why muddy the waters of Lake Langley with this website? Seems a bit hypocritical, I know. The thing is, the Langley saga is multifaceted, and some of those facets shine brighter than others. My intent here is to create the most streamlined, and dare I say, entertaining version of the narrative, one that can be enjoyed by newcomer and aficionado alike. If nothing else I aim to satisfy myself. Hence the cherry-picked nature of the information presented. Sure, this results in some contradictions between sources, but only to highlight "differences served by memories shared," as Evans would put it. As far as my version of the story being "true," I feel there are human truths contained within, as there are in any story. Consider it a remix, if you will, or a collage. Did you see Donald Barthelme's obituary? He said that collage was the art form of the 20th century.

That being said, I must lead off with a disclaimer. I do not claim ownership of copyright over any of the materials reproduced within. This site is presented for "edutainment" purposes only (because why should you pay when it comes from the heart?). Also, I feel it falls under the umbrella of fair use as a derivative work. Like Richard Prince before me, I contest that re-appropriation constitutes an entirely new work of art in and of itself. Unlike Richard Prince, however, I do not profit from said art. This website generates no income (in fact, it costs me money) and the entirety of its text is available as a free PDF download. So disseminate at will.

And, if I may, on a more personal note, I believe art is therapy. It was my psychiatrist who suggested I not only write, but (most importantly) write about other people, in an effort to curb what she describes as "narcissistic tendencies." And those other people have to be REAL people, because, according to my psychiatrist (who is NOT a writer, but no matter), writing fiction is just another way of writing about oneself. Finally, and this is the most relevant bit, I have to SHARE that writing with other people. (I have a doctor's note to back this up. A literal prescription to write.)

So, in closing, to the respective publishers and copyright holders of *Breakfast with the Monolith, The Paradox Twins, The Third Twin,* and any other related works, please—don't sue my ass. Or the rest of me, for that matter. None of my body parts have that kind of money. Unless, of course, you take into account their current value on the black market, although I'd rather not have to resort to that.

And if you do decide to litigate, please know, I have taken the necessary precautions to conceal my identity from prying eyes with ill intentions. I know The Powers That Be take pride in probing all my secret moves, but remember—I, the artist, am the maker of rules, and it is THEY who are the fools.

But enough about me. We're here to talk about the Langleys, one of the most fascinating American families of the modern age. So strap in and enjoy the rocket ride.

T-minus ten...

The Webmaster[1]
Joshua Chaplinsky (a pseudonym)[2]

2016

[1] All footnotes conceived and composed by the Webmaster.
I didn't want to bog down the main text with my editorializing and cultural cross-references, so here you will find all the necessary supplemental information to help you fully understand the depth and breadth of this work. If this document as a whole represents the story of the Langley family, then consider the footnotes my modest contribution to said story. Better yet, consider them a role I fill within the narrative itself. Because as I have learned, if one spends enough time on the periphery, they will inevitably find themselves drawn into the Langley's orbit.

[2] Even though I choose to employ a pseudonym, all other names have been changed to preserve the truth. Since *Breakfast with the Monolith* and its screenplay adaptations are technically fiction, I've taken the liberty of changing the names that were changed to protect the privacy of the people the characters were based on back to their actual names—in order to avoid any confusion within the narrative of this website.

BREAKFAST WITH THE MONOLITH by MAX LANGLEY

THE DAWN OF MAN

The sunrise peaks over the edge of Newton-Wellesley Hospital, painting a pastel orange streak across the sky. Wisps of cirrus cloud provide depth and texture as the soft light intensifies. Crystallized moisture refracts incoming photons, sending beams of light shooting in all directions. An outsider happening upon such a display might wonder: Are these atmospheric phenomena typical of a New England morning, or an auspicious herald of the day to come?

Though erected in the late 19th Century, the interior of the brick edifice is an austere 60s modern. White floors, white walls, white molded furniture. The designers had intended for the decor to give off the impression of cleanliness, but these days it only serves to make dirt and stains stand out all the more.

Off in a quiet corner of the waiting area, Paul Langley sits rigid in his chair, thumbing through an old issue of LIFE Magazine. The cover features the Gemini space capsule afloat in choppy green water. Paul's buzzcut matches that of John Young, the returning astronaut who awaits assistance from Navy frogmen. Paul wears a dark suit, standard attire for an academic of the time period. He does not so much inhabit the clothing as it confines him.

Like satellites in Paul's orbit, a pack of chimps mill about the waiting room. Their suits, while loose and ill-fitting, are indicative of the time as well. Paul glances at his watch, surveys the docile primates with indifference.

Through a pair of double doors and down the hall, in a sterile room lit fluorescent bright, his wife Florence is in the process of giving birth to their first child. She leans forward in bed, nightgown soaked with sweat. She forces breath in and out of clenched teeth. A doctor appears from between her legs.

"It won't be long now, Mrs. Langley. How are we holding up?"

She nods her head furiously, sending droplets of perspiration flying in all directions.

"Alright, one more push should do the trick. Are we ready?"

Florence shakes her head left to right, scattering more sweat.

"I can't..."

The doctor gives a patronizing smile from beneath his surgical mask. His voice never loses its even tone.

"That's not what your body's telling me, Mrs. Langley, and your body's the one in charge here. So when I give the signal, you're gonna push, Okay? Ready? And... push!"

Florence grunts and pushes. Her grunt morphs into a protracted bellow. Just as she's about to give up, there is a welcome release of pressure and a thin cry cuts the air. The doctor holds up a small, wet infant. Despite the exertion, the new mother's lips form an involuntary smile.

The smile turns quizzical as a nurse hands the doctor a blue rubber bulb, which he jams into the newborn's nostrils and throat to slurp out the epithelial plugs and excess amniotic fluid. But this oddity is soon forgotten as the doctor places the child in its mother's arms for the first time and bonding commences.

Back in the waiting room, both Paul and the chimps look up in expectation as the doctor bursts through a pair of doors, spattered with blood.

"Congratulations, Mr. Langley..." The doctor pauses for dramatic effect, a flourish he's refined over hundreds of births and considers his signature. "It's a boy."

Paul is put off by the gore, even from across the room. Despite this he gives a single, emphatic nod of approval. The previously passive chimps go wild. Ape-shit, if you will. One of them produces a box from which it distributes cigars, which the others proceed to throw, eat, and/or jam into every available orifice.

A nurse appears out of nowhere to help Paul into a green surgical mask and smock. She ushers him down the hall and into the delivery room where he finds Florence cradling their newborn son. The smile, which hasn't left her face, widens at the sight of her husband, the father of her child. He acknowledges her with a less emphatic nod than he gave the doctor, pushing against the nurse's hand at the small of his back, maintaining his distance from the goo-smeared lump of flesh.

The moment is short-lived, however, as Florence clutches her stomach and cries out.

"Everything alright, Mrs. Langley?" the doctor asks, his face devoid of concern.

Florence takes a deep breath and exhales slow, riding out the wave of pain.

"It feels like I'm having another contraction."

The doctor poo-poos the idea with a wave of his hand.

"I wouldn't worry, those are just after pains. They're completely normal."

"It really hurts."

The doctor mock-rolls his eyes, smiles at Paul.

"You can always tell the first timers, am I right?"

Paul cracks a perfunctory half-smile. The doctor turns back to Florence.

"I'll take a look, if it'll make you feel any better."

He pulls on a fresh rubber glove and reaches a casual hand between Florence's legs. His smile fades as he gropes around inside her.

"Nurse? Get my mitt. We're going into extra innings."

A nurse whisks the infant away from its mother and deposits it in Paul's arms. Immediately the child starts to wail. Paul holds it at arm's length like a burnt roast.

"What's happening?" Florence yells over the confusion. The doctor leans towards her, over her abdomen, so he doesn't have to shout.

"Mrs. Langley, this may come as a surprise to you, but you're about to have twins."

"Twins?" She repeats the word as if she doesn't grasp its meaning.

"Nothing to worry about. You're already an old pro at this." The doctor repositions himself between her legs. "Ready? On the count of—"

But she is already pushing. Paul looks on in horror as the miracle of life unfolds before his eyes. An instant replay of events he'd intentionally opted out of the first time.

"That's taking the initiative!" the doctor yells, pumping a fist in the air.

The yell echoes down the hall and out into the waiting room, where the chimps continue to scream, shake their fists, and destroy furniture in primal celebration. In a surprising turn of events, some of them have even managed to light their cigars.

Back in the delivery room, the sound of rioting chimps blends with Florence's screams. The doctor doesn't seem to pay it any mind. He turns and gives Paul a reassuring wink from between Florence's legs.

Off that wink, like the doctor is some sort of obstetric Barbara Eden, a pack of screaming chimps magically appear, filling the room. Some wear nurses uniforms and others scrubs. The odd hairy ass is exposed by open-backed hospital gown. Paul watches in disbelief as they jump up and down, throw equipment, and generally wreak havoc. One sticks a glass thermometer in its ear while another guzzles a bottle of rubbing alcohol.

The chaos overwhelms Paul's mind. His consciousness disengages from his corporeal being, and he finds himself floating outside his own body. A body which has been replaced by a man-sized monolith. The fugue of "Requiem" by Gyorgy Ligeti emanates from the matte black slab. The chimps and Florence continue to scream. The doctor continues to take no notice.

Paul doesn't know what he finds more distressing: the howling primates, his out of body experience, or the bird's eye view of a crowning child. He takes a small amount of comfort in the fact that the throwing of feces has yet to be engaged in—and that's when his wife loses control of her bowels. If Paul's floating consciousness had a stomach, it would have emptied its contents onto the floor. The pilot light on his sexual attraction to his wife is blown out by a sputtering fart.

Then, after what feels like an eternity, a small cry cuts the air. It silences the rest of the noise, including the wails of the child in Paul's arms. Paul's consciousness snaps back inside his body and he is once again a man, no longer a monolith. He scans the delivery room and the chimps are nowhere to be seen.

The doctor looks up from between Florence's legs, puzzled.

"What is it?" Florence manages between gulps of air.

"It's... another boy."

The doctor holds up a second infant by its feet. A small vestigial tail twitches back and forth as the child announces its arrival to the world[3].

---

[3] Only twenty-three cases of a human child born with a tail have been recorded since the late 1800s. Most likely before that time they were considered the spawn of Satan and promptly burned alive. My own research produced no official record of either Langley twin being born with such a physical anomaly.

STATE OF

REPORT OF BIRTH *

Form 206 A

VITAL STATISTICS DEPARTMENT—COUNTY CLERK'S OFFICE

1. Full Name of Child _T.B.D. — Langley_
2. Sex _Male_   Race or Color (if not of the white race)
3. Number of Child of this Mother   How many now living (in all) _1_
4. Date of this Birth _March 17, 1965_
5. Place of Birth, No. _Newton_ Street _Wellesley Hospital_   Village / City / Town
6. Residence of Mother No.   Street
7. Place of Birth   TOWN   STATE OR COUNTRY   AGE OF
   a. Father _Fall River, MA_   _32_
   b. Mother _MA_   _25_
8. Full Name of Mother _Florence Langley_
9. Maiden Name of Mother _Wheatley_
10. Full Name of Father _Paul Langley_
11. Occupation of Father _Maintenance_
12. Name and Address of Nurse or Attendant (if any) _Penelope Winsland_

Date _March 17, 19 65_   Reported by _Dr. Valentin_   Residence   Telephone

* Still births should be reported on a separate blank form.
‡ The baptismal or christian name of child should be certified, if possible, when this certificate is made, and should, in any case, be reported to the County Clerk within a year.
† In case of more than one child at a birth, a SEPARATE RETURN must be made for each, and the number of each, in order of birth, stated _# and male child — SEE ATTACHED_

4

---

[4] There are official, typed birth certificates on record for both Langley twins that include full names and times of birth, but there is also this—hastily written in the delivery room, presumably before twin #2 came calling. At first I read Occupation of Father as "scientist," but upon closer inspection, I believe it says "maintenance." I'm not 100% on Paul Langley's employment timeline or what year he earned his PhD, but I found this an interesting detail. Reminds me of a friend who was told throughout his childhood that his father was the Chief of Police in their home county, when in reality the man had been a supermarket security guard.

Here's a fun bit of trivia: Massachusetts has one of the highest rates of twin births in the nation, approximately thirty-eight out of every thousand. That's a lot of doppelgangers. *The Boston Globe* attributes this to large clusters of rich white ladies with easy access to fertility treatment putting off reproduction until after they've established their career.

BREAKFAST WITH THE MONOLITH -
DAVID RYAN - 5/22/14 DRAFT

EXT. LANGLEY HOUSE - NIGHT

TITLE CARD: "38 YEARS LATER"[5]

The bright, white dot of JUPITER is
visible in the night sky, accompanied
by Johann Strauss's "THE BLUE DANUBE".

INT. LIVING ROOM - NIGHT

A framed PHOTO adorns the mantelpiece--the
Langley twins as toddlers, sitting in
a sandbox. One plays with a toy ROCKET,
which obscures the face of the other.

A drunken PAUL LANGLEY (70's), stag-
gers by, bottle in hand, and acci-
dently knocks the photo off the ledge.

---

[5] A feature retained throughout most drafts of the *Breakfast with the Monolith* screenplay adaptation is the use of title cards similar to those found in Stanley Kubrick's *2001: A Space Odyssey*. Aside from the one footnoted above, they are exactly the same as in the film (minus the "Intermission" card). In Kubrick's film, the second title card reads, "Jupiter Mission: 18 Months Later," not "38 Years Later," but as you will see, having Paul Langley die 18 months after the birth of the twins would wreak havoc on the story's timeline. Even as presented here, following the excerpt from *Breakfast with the Monolith*, it doesn't work perfectly, as Paul Langley died closer to 45 years after the birth of his sons.

EXT. LANGLEY HOUSE - NIGHT

Paul wanders out into the front yard.
He takes a swig and stares up into
the expanse of the sky.

His body sways, head leaned back as if asleep
on his feet. Jupiter gives a sly wink.

The bottle falls out of his hand, hits
the ground with a dull thud. A tear
leaks from the corner of his eye.

DISSOLVE TO:

EXT. LANGLEY HOUSE - DAY

Paul stares at the sky, still on his
feet, frozen in time.

MILLIE BLACKFORD (19), a literal and
figurative Girl Next Door, shoulders a
backpack and exits the adjacent house.
She wears a crop top and tight jeans.[6]

---

[6] If this movie ever gets made, I think Neil deGrasse Tyson, amateur film critic that he is, will have something to say about Millie's wardrobe in this scene, since the best visibility for Jupiter in the night sky at this time of day in the Northeast is during the dead of Winter.

                    MILLIE
                (calls out)
            Morning, Mr. Langley.

She gets no response.

                    MILLIE (CONT'D)
            Mr. Langley?

She makes her way over and tentatively touches his arm.

                    MILLIE (CONT'D)
            Are you alright?

The body falls forward in a slow
motion arc and Paul Langley collides
with the ground, face first.

                              SMASH CUT TO:

INT. CORONER'S OFFICE - DAY

CU: PAUL LANGLEY'S SMASHED FACE

ALAN[7] LANGLEY (45), paunchy and unkempt,
studies his dead father on the slab.

---

[7] Albert Langley goes by Alan in his everyday life. A man of many
names is a man after my own heart.

OBITUARY: BOSTON GLOBE

PAUL LANGLEY — 1934 - 2010

Prominent physicist Paul Langley died peacefully at his Newton Massachusetts home late in the evening on Monday February 22nd. He was 76 years old.

Born in 1934 in Fall River, Massachusetts, to working class parents, he developed a love for science early on. As a boy he would spend his summers at the local library, devouring books. At the age of ten, he became the youngest person to compete at the high school level of the Massachusetts State Science and Engineering Fair when he lied about his age on the entry form. The offense resulted in instant disqualification, but the judges took notice.

Despite an exemplary scholastic record he dropped out of school to manage his ailing father's electronics business. After his father's passing, he continued his education parttime, and would go on to earn his GED and undergraduate degree from Bristol Community College. Based on his work there, with the aid of grants and scholarships, he was accepted to MIT, where he graduated with a PhD in Physics. After years of work in both the public and private sector, including a stint as a data analyst for NASA, he returned to his alma mater as a professor. He retired from teaching in 1984.[8]

He is survived by his former-wife, Florence Langley, and their two sons: Max Langley, renowned author of the bestselling Anthropica book series for young adults; and Albert Langley, local high school science teacher.

Private services will be held at Heywood Funeral Home in Newton on Monday, March 1st, followed by burial at Oak Grove Cemetery in Fall River.

---

[8] "Retired." *The Globe*, playing nice, as opposed to the obituary in the more tabloid-leaning *Herald*.

NEWTON POLICE DEPARTMENT:
INCIDENT REPORT

At approximately 6:30 AM on February 22nd,
2010, the officer on duty responded to a 911 call
reporting the discovery of a dead body. Officer
arrived to find male decedent face down on ground
with what appeared to be a broken nose and facial
bruising, an empty bottle of liquor beside him. Millicent Blackford, the young woman who made the
call, identified the man as Paul Langley. She came
upon the body after exiting her home that morning
(she and her mother live next door). She witnessed
the decedent standing in the yard, at which point
she called his name. When he didn't respond, she
walked over and touched his arm, prompting the
body to fall forward, resulting in the facial injuries.

Paramedics arrived and performed emergency
procedures. They then transported the body to
Newton-Wellesley Hospital for a doctor to make
a declaration of death. The officer made several
attempts to contact next of kin at this time.[9]

Finding the front door open, the officer conducted
a preliminary search of the premises. The interior

---

[9] An interesting detail that could potentially explain, in a non-supernat-
ural way, certain unanswered questions in Albert Langley's *The Paradox
Twins*, re: how Mrs. Langley first became aware of her husband's passing.

of the home exhibited complete disarray.
Numerous empty liquor bottles littered the floor
and the air smelled of rotten garbage, but the
officer found no indication of foul play. The door
showed no signs of forced entry.

AUTOPSY REPORT

NAME: Langley, Paul   CASE NUMBER: 6651415
DATE OF DEATH: February 22, 2010
AGE: 76   RACE: White   SEX: Male

INVESTIGATING AGENCY: Newton Police Department

DATE AND TIME OF AUTOPSY: February, 25, 2010 at 9:27AM

AUTOPSY FINDINGS

1.Nasal Fracture

Both right and left nasal bones exhibit numerous fractures, accompanied on the surface by facial bruising. Damage to cartilage of the nasal septum also evident.

2. Osteopenia and muscle atrophy

Subject exhibits lower than average bone mineral density, bordering on osteoporosis, as well as excessive muscular atrophy, consistent with immobility or an extremely sedentary lifestyle.

3. Dilated cardiomyopathy

The heart exhibits a damaged myocardium and the function of the left ventricular pump seems to be impaired.

4. Marked coronary atherosclerosis

Coronary arteries contain moderate fatty buildup, not inconsistent with subjects age or lifestyle.

5. Pulmonary edema

Moderate accumulation of fluid exhibited in the subject's left and right lung.

6. Fluid redistribution

Noted in the upper extremities as well as in the appearance of facial swelling.

7. Diverticulosis

Noted presence of non-inflamed diverticula in subject's colon. Noted deterioration in muscle of colon wall.

8. Minimal decomposition

Subject displays minimal decomposition, consistent with time of discovery and temperature at time of death.

9. Toxicology (complete report forthcoming)

BAC of 0.273, RBC well below the average norm.

CAUSE OF DEATH: arteriosclerotic cardiovascular disease
MANNER OF DEATH: natural [10]

---

[10] Osteopenia and muscle atrophy, coincidentally, are both also adverse effects of long-term weightlessness. (See also: *Spaceflight osteopenia*.) So is facial swelling due to fluid distribution, AKA moon face.

Other known side effects of space travel consistent with cardiovascular disease and alcoholism include: poor circulation, decreased red blood cell production, and a compromised immune system. As revealed by his autopsy, Paul Langley's body exhibited all of the above.

THE THIRD TWIN
by MILLICENT BLACKFORD

—For my mother and father. This book is my attempt to get to know you better.

I'd just had another fight with mom.

Same one we always had. More of a recurring nightmare, really, where I stood outside myself and watched powerless as we rehashed the same old arguments, neither of us making any headway. I don't even remember how it started. There we were, having a perfectly pleasant dinner, when all of a sudden we were talking about Dad.

Don't get me wrong, my mother's a saint. She raised me single-handedly on a librarian's salary and I never wanted for anything. I didn't even know we were "poor" until I got older. I thought all families had giant hunks of cheese and boxes of powdered milk delivered to their doorstep every week. So no complaints there. But any time I broached the subject of my father she transformed into a different woman. Like when someone uttered the secret word on *Pee-Wee's Playhouse*. As soon as I said "Dad" the air filled with screams and the furniture started going ape-shit.

She'd mellowed with age, but still. I didn't enter into the conversation lightly. I thought for sure once I turned old enough she'd put her hands over my eyes and lead me out into the driveway, like one of those brats on *My Super Sweet 16*. She'd pull her hands away to reveal the man I'd never known—*Surprise! Your first car is your absentee father!* Instead, when I turned that magical age, we had one of our biggest blowouts ever, ruining my surprise birthday party. After that, she never threw me another. The year I turned twenty-one, I didn't even bother bringing up Dad. I got drunk with some friends instead.

This past year I turned twenty-five, so maybe it had been too long and we were overdue. Maybe she felt like she hadn't properly celebrated my birthday these past years by not getting into it. Felt like she'd been neglecting me, neglecting some sort of dysfunctional tradition. Or maybe she needed to reassure herself I hadn't gone off and found out on my own. Either way, that night was fight night, and I retreated to my room to nurse my wounds before the food even had a chance to cool.

To make matters worse, I had a writing assignment due the next day, and that sure as hell wasn't getting done. Some creatives thrive on conflict, can't produce art without it. Me, I internalize and shut down. So I flopped into bed with my tattered copy of *Left Hand of Darkness* and started reading, willing myself to dream about the Hainish universe. Instead I had a dream about my father.

I know, dream sequences. Is there any bigger clichè? Dreams are such a big part of life—they say you have them every night whether you remember them or not—but rarely do they provide the mineable subtext they do in books and film. Maybe that's why no one's ever captured the authenticity of a real dream. They don't make for interesting narrative unless you zazz them up with backwards talking little people.

Anyway, I dreamt my mother had her hands over my eyes as she led me out in front of the house for a birthday surprise, like I'd always wanted. Only, I wasn't sixteen. More like five or six. I remember feeling nervous like a child, like when the doctor tells you to look away when you know he's about to give you a shot. I knew the details of my dream surprise, and that was the root of my anxiety.

My mother pulled her hands away with a flourish and there he stood—my father—only he had his back to me. I leaned back into my mother, not wanting to approach him, but she gave me a little pat on the bottom and a push towards the man. I stared down at patent leather shoes as I inched forward, my sullen reflection staring back at me. The curve of the shoes distorted my features, making me look exactly how I felt at the moment. I continued this way across the driveway, a never ending expanse of bleached concrete, step by tiny step.

Only when I finally looked up did I see he stood right there in front of me. I turned back to my mother, a mere five or six feet behind me, unsure of what to do next. She just nodded and smiled, nodded and smiled. I turned back to my father. Reached out a hand and tugged his pant leg. He turned around. I looked up.

I couldn't see his face due to the harsh backlight of the sun. No, his face *was* the sun, shining into my eyes, causing me to blink. You know the movie poster for John Carpenter's *The Thing*? It looked like that (*sans* parka). Spots danced before my eyes and I had to avert my gaze.

I looked down at my feet, our toes almost touching. In my shoes, his face didn't reflect as the sun, but as an actual face. Even more distorted than my own had been, stretched thin and tied in knots. Mouth howling in silence. Antarctic-research-station cold crept into my bones, despite the sun.

That's when I woke up.

Of course, the whole thing wasn't as linear as all that. It was fluid, every moment occurring and reoccurring on an endless loop in a fraction of a second. My parents were colors and fear was a blanket of smoke, if that makes any sense (I know, it doesn't).

So I was already unnerved by the dream and by the fight I'd had with mom when I walked outside that morning. And when I saw Mr. Langley standing there, his back to me, I wanted to run back inside and curl up in bed. When I called his name and he didn't answer, I wanted to scream to someone else for help. Instead I found my feet moving forward of their own accord, step by tiny step. I found my hand reaching out to touch his shoulder, although I felt like a child reaching for the hem of his pants. And I don't know what I expected to happen when I touched him—maybe he'd turn around, scoop me up in his arms and tell me he'd missed me, walk me back over to my house as I clung to his neck—but instead he fell forward in slow motion, hitting the ground with such force that I stumbled back, dropped onto the seat of my pants and cried.[11]

---

[11] One of the great things about Millie Blackford's writing is that she really makes you feel for her characters. Granted, this character is a real person—her—which might in some subconscious way influence those feelings. I am not a particularly empathetic person by nature, but that doesn't change the fact that this passage makes me want to reach inside the narrative and put my arms around her. It's one of the many reasons I consider her my favorite author.

THE PARADOX TWINS
by ALBERT LANGLEY

*Dedicated to the son of my mother, that snarled and clawed
in her womb. I know thee and love thee, brother.*
— *"The Twins" by Aleister Crowley*

It was Millie Blackford who discovered my father dead on
his feet, the poor girl. Right around the time my 9AM
physics class attempted to wrap their collective heads
around the concept of geometric gravity.

Bear with me, there's a correlation.

As I explained to my students that morning, whether
it's Newton's apple, Einstein's falling man, or the heads
of bored high schoolers hitting their desks, the observed
attraction between two masses is a result of the warping
of spacetime, not a force exerted by the objects themselves. And although disgruntled coworkers and estranged
family members often described my father as a "force of
nature," and Millie's touch set his body in motion, it was
the warping of the fabric of the universe that brought his
already stiff body crashing to the ground with an audible
breaking of bones.

But this isn't a science lesson. Because although science
enters into my story, there are some things I can't back up
with empirical evidence. Like my mother's premonitions.
And the Spaceman.

But that comes later.

The class raised their heads in unison at the principal's
knock. They watched as he and I conversed in the hall,
waiting like a silent movie audience for the interstitials.

But they didn't need words to get the gist of our conversation. My face gave it away. I could tell by the silence that greeted me upon my return.

"My apologies," I told them. "But it looks like we're going to have to cut class short today."

They did me the courtesy of not bursting into cheers until after I left the room.

—

I drove straight to the medical examiner's office to identify the body. He called the death "unremarkable" but recommended an autopsy anyway. It had only been a few days since I'd last seen Dad, but I almost didn't recognize him. His paper thin skin bordered on translucent, body shrunken to the point of desiccation. Duncan MacDougall once claimed the human soul had a mass of twenty-one grams, measurable upon death, but my father looked like he had lost twenty-one pounds.

"Well?" the examiner said, anxious to get back to the sack lunch all coroners seem to have waiting in the wings on such occasions. I focused on the firework display of burst capillaries on my father's nose, as unique as any fingerprint.

"Yeah, that's him."

I'd like to point out as a side note that although it can aggravate it, drinking is not the primary cause of rosacea. That being said, my father had aggravated the shit out of it.

In our younger years, my brother and I would often quote old W.C. Fields routines behind Dad's back. Me (in my squeaky, pre-pubescent voice): *Mommy, doesn't that man have a funny nose?* Max (doing his best dowdy marm): *You mustn't make fun. You'd like to have a nose like that full of nickels, wouldn't you?*

But as we got older, good old fashioned shame replaced our wisecracking. Before he stopped making an effort to keep up appearances, my father would apply my mother's concealer to his nose, to soften the glare, which only made his condition that much more obvious, that much sadder. It was a relief when he became more reclusive and stopped wearing makeup.

———

With that bit of unpleasantness out of the way, I retreated to the safety of my studio apartment. (The real unpleasantness would begin the next day, with the probating of my father's will.) I didn't consider my digs pathetic at the time, but that's the thing about bachelor pads—you don't realize you're living in one until it's too late.[12] In retrospect, I represented the quintessential pathetic bachelor. In the decade or so I'd lived there, no woman had ever graced my home with her presence. I kept the apartment OCD clean but sparsely furnished. I had a microwave, a TV, and a sofa bed—that's it. I subsisted on TV dinners and takeout. When I got home from work I'd grade papers for a couple hours, then I'd turn on the TV and switch off my brain, which is exactly what I

---

[12] Ouch. The cruel stigma of the unmarried man living on his own. The final frontier of marginalized groups it is still acceptable to discriminate against. Here is a perfect example of the damaging self-hatred it can instill.

proceeded to do that night. I didn't want to process what had happened. I wanted to forget.

And forget I did—to set my alarm. I woke up on the couch the next morning, already late to meet the lawyer. I didn't even have time to wash up. I grabbed my keys and ran out the door in the previous day's clothes.

—

The probating of my father's will was overseen by his lawyer of choice, a slimy bit of mustache in a cheap suit named Todd Barnett (name changed to protect the slimy). As I sat across from him I thought about how punchable his face was. I imagined his oily complexion as an evolutionary adaptation that served the same purpose as the Vaseline a cutman applies to a boxer. He pushed a stack of papers towards me.

"It's pretty cut and dry. He left everything to you."

My eyes scanned the documents.

"That's because he knew no one else would give a shit."

He couldn't argue with that. Dad's decision was a purely practical one. Based on years of my guilt-induced predictability—making sure he had groceries, making sure his utilities didn't get cut off, making sure he still *lived*. Ironic, then, that he'd shuffled off this mortal coil during one of the few moments I had my back turned. Bastard.

Todd waited out my reverie with patience. He gave me a knowing grin, a grin gift wrapped with a bow. God, I wanted to punch him.

"And how *is* your brother these days?"

Punchpunchpunchpunchpunchpunchpunchpunch.

"Haven't spoken to him."

That would have been enough for most normal people, but Todd wasn't normal, or a person. He was a piece of shit, and I could see he enjoyed my discomfort. He twisted the knife a little more. It felt like a dull letter opener.

"Do you expect him at the funeral?"

"That depends on whether or not it fits into his busy schedule."

Todd slapped an open palm against his desk, as if having a *eureka!* moment.

"That's right, the new book. My kids love his stuff."

He said it like he was paying *me* a compliment. Next thing you know, he'd be asking me to procure autographed copies for his brats. I took a break from my scanning to glare. Bad move. I played right into Todd's hands.

"You've never gotten over the fact I represented your father in the divorce, have you?"

"Let's not forget that ridiculous suit against the university."

"He was a tenured professor who was the victim of unlawful termination."

"He was having an affair with one of his students!"

Thick silence filled the room. Silence you could cut with a dull letter opener. Lucky for us Todd happened to have one. He pressed the figurative blade against my throat, a clerical Sweeney Todd.

"A *consensual* affair with *an adult*. Did it hurt you that much to see the old man keep his pension?" He pointed at the papers in my hands. "You're the one who's benefiting."

Benefiting? I wanted to scream. *You call this indignity from beyond the grave a benefit?* But instead of launching into another rebuttal, I bit my tongue. I signed the documents without another word and high-tailed it out of his office.

——

Dad's funeral took place two days later, the burial an understated affair. Aside from the few colleagues my father hadn't completely alienated, attendees included Slimy Todd, myself, Millie, and Millie's mother. I didn't know the minister personally, but whoever he was, he'd done his homework.

"Being a scientist, Paul Langley didn't believe in an afterlife. He didn't define immortality as perpetual linear existence, but something that resided outside of time, in the infinite possibilities of quantum physics. As I'm sure most of you know, that's about as close to a belief system as he got."

The crowd gave a polite chuckle, like when you describe a real pain-in-the-ass as "intense" or "methodical."

"But seriously, folks…"

I tuned out and looked over at Millie. Poor girl wouldn't even be here if she hadn't discovered the body. Probably felt bad about breaking Dad's face. Although thinking about it now, she might've done him a favor. Methinks all the king's men reconstructed my father's nose based on a photo from his younger years. And the makeup job… Let's just say they put Dad's concealer application skills to shame.

But we were talking about Millie. She wore a plain black dress, the type of multi-purpose garment that worked as well for cocktail parties as it did for funerals. Not that I'd been to many of either. I could hear my father's voice from beyond the grave. *She wears that dress like toast wears butter.* Millie looked up as if she'd heard it too, and I averted my gaze. I caught Mrs. Blackford's follow-up scowl from the corner of my eye. Had they both heard it? I admonished my father for saying such an inappropriate thing, especially at a time like this.

The minister droned on.

...pillar of the community...father figure to aspiring scientists...dedicated family man...

God, this guy laid it on thick. You'd think he got paid by the word.

Fast forward to handshakes and condolences, the awkward smiles of those who don't know what they're supposed to say. Beyond the well-wishers, I noticed a man leaning against a tree with effortless nonchalance as he watched the proceedings. I didn't remember seeing him at the burial itself. Somebody's driver? A bodyguard? Who the hell did I know that needed a bodyguard? The guy looked to be in great physical shape, like every other guy my age seemed to these days. I gave a wave and he nodded in return.

"Would you excuse me, please?" I extricated myself from the small group of mourners around me. The stranger met me halfway.

"Hello, brother," he said.

—

Like so many Americans, I tend to stress eat when depressed. And seeing Max after all these years made me extremely depressed. Especially since we used to be identical. Maybe we'd spent too much time apart, because a noticeable change had taken place. I knew it wasn't some sort of cognitive disconnect on my part, because we weren't getting the usual amount of double takes one expects when two of the same guy sit across from each other in a restaurant. Him picking at a salad while I wolfed down a burger and fries didn't help, either.

"I almost didn't recognize you," I said, stating the obvious. Fuck the pleasantries. We'd barely said a word since the cemetery. After crashing our father's funeral he told me we needed to talk, so to buy myself some panic time I faked a call from the funeral director and told Max I'd catch up with him.

"It *has* been ten years," he said.

Like I didn't know. Like *he* didn't know I knew.

"You make it sound like I don't look in the mirror every morning." I took a huge chug from my pint of beer.

"There's a lot to be said for lifestyle choice."

I slammed the glass on the table, wiped the foam from my lips.

"I forgot. You only go to bars to write."

Max shrugged. "Beats going to AA."

Max was a firm non-believer in a higher power. He credited writing for his sobriety, which kind of made writing his higher power, except he didn't want to deify it—he wanted to deify himself. The writer as almighty creator, wishing worlds into existence like stars in the sky.

"I wouldn't know. I have a little thing called self control." I shoved burger into my face. Off my burger—

"When was your last physical?" He did me the courtesy of not raising a finely manicured eyebrow and looking me up and down in an exaggerated manner. I stopped mid chew, dropped burger rind onto my plate.

"Is this what you came back for?"

I could see a million potential comebacks racing around behind his eyes, like an olde-tyme stock ticker under a glass dome. Max could volley insults all day. Which is why it surprised me to see his face soften so early in the argument.

"You're right," he said. "I apologize."

The thing you need to know about Max is, he never truly felt remorse. He played possum, but only when it benefitted him. I decided to change the subject.

"Where are you staying?" I resumed a slow chew. The lump of ground beef had gone cold in my mouth. *Bolus.* I couldn't stop thinking the word. *Bolus.* The more I thought it the weirder it sounded. *That's me, the human bolus. A cold glob of meat sitting on a tongue.*

"The publisher put me up in a hotel, but I thought I could stay at the house if it's alright with you."

Alarm bells went off in my head. I tried to think of a good excuse over the clamor.

"I don't know… the place is a mess."

"That's cool. I'm only in town for a couple days. I can slum it." He flagged down a passing waiter. "Check, please."

I considered making a show of fighting him over the bill, but I'd had my fill of petty conflict for one day. He didn't let my pride off the hook, though.

"Don't worry, this one's on the publisher."

I stewed over that little jab the whole ride back to the house, thinking of ways to get Max back. We didn't speak the entire ride, because he still had his limo for another hour and he never wasted a chance to flaunt his success. I had hoped he'd take his time, tour the old neighborhood so I could beat him back and have the chance to clean up a bit, but he pulled up right after me. We got out of our respective vehicles[13] and approached the house in silence. I unlocked the front door and let it swing inward. Max took in the clutter.

"Holy shit, you weren't kidding."

I felt every dirty dish, every empty beer bottle his eyes touched. The skyscraper piles of newspaper, the unwashed clothes. All of it.

"I'm gonna have to take a week off work to get the place market ready." I led the way into the house, tip-toeing through the debris.

"You're gonna sell?"

"Todd's already lined up a buyer. He's a scumbag, but he's a good lawyer."

Max nodded in agreement.

"Remember when he got Dad off—"

"I remember." I didn't need to be reminded of that story

---

[13] According to the DMV database, which employs laughable security encryption, Alan still drives the same dented up Saturn he always has.

twice in one week. For me the embarrassment it caused bordered on excruciating. Max shared the anecdote like someone bragging about a relative's Purple Heart.

He walked over to the mantelpiece and picked up a framed photo of us as kids, the only one on display in the entire house. Me and Max as toddlers, fighting over a toy rocket.[14] A lightning bolt crack cut across the glass, dividing the picture in half—me on one side, him on the other. The toy obscured one of our faces, I couldn't tell which. My father used to say it didn't matter because we both had the same face.

"I don't suppose I get any say in the matter?" Max asked.

I took the picture out of his hand and placed it back on the mantel. I made a mental note to get a new frame.

"Maybe if you'd helped me play zookeeper all these years..." A low blow, but I'd take the point. A flurry of quick jabs followed.

"Come on, that's not fair."

"Oh yeah? To who?"

"To me. You were the favorite, which is why you get to deal with all the bullshit."

"Oh, please. Saying Dad favored anyone is like comparing apples to... slightly less insignificant apples."

"He didn't throw *you* out of the house."

"You could have come back any time. He could barely remember his own name, let alone banishing you from his kingdom."

---

[14] A photo which featured heavily in the promotion of Alan's book, but not Max's.

This wasn't technically true. We both knew a good, mean drunk will always remember exactly what they need to make you feel like shit.

"I was going through my own dark time, remember?" Max paused so I could. "I didn't want to endanger my own sobriety."

I sighed. I couldn't argue with that. Only a jerk would argue with that. I never wanted to be a jerk more in my life.

"We aren't getting off to a very good start, are we?"

He flashed his smug grin for the umpteenth time that night. Like he practiced it in the mirror.

"I'd say it's par for the course." The man didn't have a sincere bone in his whole body.

"Look, it's been a long day," I told him. "We can talk more in the morning."

—

I let Max take the guest room—the only room in the house not trashed. For some reason I couldn't let him see Dad's room in its current state. It looked like it had been hit by a tornado. A very drunk tornado. Books and magazines rose from the ground in towering stacks. A sea of dirty clothes littered the floor, the bed an uncharted, unmade island in its midst. I pulled back the comforter to reveal a large, dark stain.

"Great."

I pulled the sheet off the bed. The stain had gone all the way down to the mattress. I mentally crossed my fingers and flipped the thing over. More stains, but at least they had faded some.

I went through my nighttime routine, which consisted of me feeling bad while I looked at myself shirtless in the mirror. Only tonight it felt extra bad, because of Max. Somehow he had managed to escape the clutches of time. I grabbed a fistful of love handle and grimaced.

Looking back on that night, I can't help but wonder— was it a food induced nightmare? Or do I blame Max's surprise return? How about sleeping in my father's shit-stained bed? That couldn't have helped. Maybe I should cover my bases and go with all of the above. Not that it matters. All I know is, that was the first time I remember seeing the Spaceman.

Except it wasn't the Spaceman yet. At this point it was a mere presence. An androgynous shadow cloaked in darkness. I had shut the light and lay in bed, waiting for my eyes to adjust. I ran through the events of the day in my mind, cataloging the indignities, most of them at the hands of my brother. It was a long list, and I must have been more tired than I thought, because one moment I was awake and the next I had slipped into a lucid dream. The warmth drained from the room and a dark figure became visible at the foot of the bed. The outline of a person, but larger, less defined.

I stared at the figure as I continued down my list of gripes, preoccupied by my familial drama. By the time I realized something odd was happening, my shivering body had followed my mind into sleep. It felt weighed down, like I wore one of those lead blankets they use during x-rays, so your entire body isn't exposed to the radiation. I panicked and tried to push against it, sending pins and needles shooting through my limbs.

As if sensing my fear, the dark figure moved towards me. Only, it didn't actually move, it expanded, increasing its own mass by subsuming the room around it. Its nebulous border reached out in every direction at once, sucking empty bottles and dirty clothes into the void within. Piles of newspaper and magazines toppled into the darkness. Then bookshelves and other furniture as it climbed the walls. The figure grew until the ceiling became a starless night of infinite black. Then this, too, was devoured, along with my thoughts, leaving nothing.[15]

---

[15] Sounds like garden variety sleep paralysis to me, with a dash of cosmic dread. You would think an objective man of science like Alan would have realized this right away.

That said, waking dreams are a common side effect of certain anti-depressant cocktails, and are technically classified as hallucinations according to my psychiatrist, and are cause for concern if experienced on a recurring basis.

THE THIRD TWIN
by MILLICENT BLACKFORD

The first time I met Max Langley he looked like he'd just escaped a burning building in the middle of the night—a little building called the Playboy mansion.[16]

I hustled towards my car, late for class as usual. Alan stood on the lawn with a cup of coffee, staring at the spot where I'd found his father.

"Hey, Mr. Langley," I called out.

Alan's face brightened when he saw me. I steeled myself for an awkward conversation. We had chatted at the funeral, but hadn't really talked much about what had happened.

"Oh, hey Millie," he replied. "What did I tell you about that Mr. Langley business? Call me Alan. Mr. Langley was my father's…"

He trailed off when he realized where the joke was going. My heart broke a little for him. My leg started twitching, shaking the imaginary pieces down my pants.

"How is everything?" I asked, softly. He did me the favor of ignoring my nervous energy.

"Okay, all things considered. You?"

"Keepin' busy. School and stuff." Ugh. I sounded like such a teenager.

"Taking anything interesting?"

"Couple lit classes. Creative writing."

"What about science?"

---

[16] Which Max has been to on several occasions, despite being a "children's" author. Your move, J.K.!

I smiled. The latent teenager in me couldn't help it.

"Science is boring."

His face fell. Shit. Another bit of my heart crumbled and fell down my pant leg. Luckily, Max interrupted us. Lucky in that moment. If you look at it in the context of everything that came after...

He burst through the front door in a Bon Jovian[17] blaze of glory, wearing nothing but silk boxers and an open robe, also made of silk. Even though I'd seen his dust jacket photo dozens of times, I didn't recognize the man in front of me. All I saw were abs and pecs.

"Hey, Albert, where do we keep the sugar?" the abs and pecs asked.

"Albert?" I stammered. Was I staring? I was staring. I turned to Alan. Alan looked at the ground.

"Oh, I'm sorry," Max said, obviously not sorry. "I forgot, you go by *Alan* now." He turned to me. "And who's this pretty young thing?" My face went flush. The Michael Jackson song ran through my head. From before my time. Before we knew more about Michael than we wanted to.[18] Alan frowned.

"This is Mrs. Blackford's daughter, Millie. Millie, this is my brother, Max."

Max stuck out his hand. I looked up at the person attached to it and that's when it hit me.

---

[17] *Jovian*: also the adjectival form of the planet Jupiter.

[18] Ah, the dangers of hero worship. Deifying mortals is never a good idea. I met my favorite author at a reading once, and as soon as I attempted to engage them on a human level they responded with utter disdain. For my sanity's sake, I choose not to hold a grudge.

"Max Langley," he said. "Pleasure to meet you."

I put my hand in his, stunned. He had a firm grip, but soft skin. Probably from never having done a day of physical labor in his life. The dam broke and I gushed.

"I am a HUGE fan of your books. I grew up on the Anthropica series." I sounded like I'd regressed even further. I had turned twenty-five this past birthday. Technically I'd been an adult for four years. Dammit, I wanted to feel like one!

"You certainly did," he said as he looked me up and down. If I hadn't been so star struck, it would've creeped me out. "Am I going to see you at Paper and Glue tomorrow?"

Paper and Glue? I knew what those words meant separately, but together they didn't make sense. Oh wait, yes they did!

"I wish. It's sold out."

"Not a problem. I can get you in. I know a guy." He winked. It should have disgusted me. Instead—

"Oh my god, that would be so awesome, thank you!"

Max flashed the enamel.

"Then I'll see you there. It was nice meeting you, Millie."

"You too."

Max turned and rode his wave of charisma back towards the house. His back to me, he finally closed his robe, almost as an afterthought. Self-loathing flooded in. I looked at Alan. I decided to deflect the awkwardness.

"Albert? As in Einstein?"

Alan shrugged.

"My father *was* a physicist."

I glanced towards the door, to make sure Max had gone inside.

"Who's Max named after?"

"Planck."

"Never heard of him."

Alan smiled at that. I think he mistook my ignorance for a joke. To me, planks were what Max did to get his body so tight (get out of my head, abs!). Anyway, I felt bad for bringing it up. I had my own name related secret, and before I realized, I heard myself spilling it.

"If it makes you feel any better, my full name's Millicent. After my mother's sister."

"Really?" Alan's smile returned. He exuded an amazing amount of warmth when you shifted the focus away from him. It made me glad I'd told him.

"I hate it. It's an old lady name."

"I think it's nice."

"Thanks," I said, and meant it.

—

That afternoon I daydreamed my way through poly sci. I had just met *the* Max Langley. That had to be, what do you call it? Fortuitous? Serendipity? Either way, adjective or noun, it meant the same thing for me: an opportunity.

I couldn't concentrate. I decided to skip creative writing class. I had a backlog of assignments I still hadn't dealt with. Part of me began to think I'd made a mistake majoring in writing.

[Incoming rant]

First off, nobody in my class wrote anything interesting. They were all navel gazing, lint picking, masturbatory poseurs with no aspirations beyond telling their own, boring story.[19] None of them had any concept of writing as a career. They all thought they had something to say, and ironically they all said the same damn thing. It was all about me, me, ME! And God forbid you showed an interest in writing for young adults. You instantly lost all street cred. I could tell by their anemic comments they couldn't give a shit about my own work.

Plus, the teacher was some crusty old white dude on a mission to force Nabokov down the supple throats of the one or two women he accepted into his class each semester. Not exactly a nurturing environment. He had no interest in smart science fiction, but fawned over the Conan the Barbarian torture porn by the dude with the long hair who always wore the Celtic Frost t-shirt. The way that guy said the phrase, *nipples distended like pencil erasers* (and believe me, he said it a lot), gave me the heebee jeebees. (Also, did barbarians use pencils? Did they even have erasers in those supposed days?) Thankfully class took place during daylight hours, or I would've needed a security escort to my car afterwards. Nothing against metalheads, but that dude had cheerleaders chained up in his basement. Someone needed to rescue them before he ate their faces.

Ironically, the only constructive feedback came from the guy who sat in the back of the class and never said anything. His stuff was pretty good, albeit a bit experimental, and he always gave good written notes on my stories. Unfortunately he never spoke up in my defense.[20]

---

[19] She sounds like my psychiatrist here. Not sure how I feel about that...

[20] I have a sneaking suspicion he probably regrets this.

[End rant]

But knowing Max Langley, one of the biggest selling YA authors of all time, that meant something. Plus, he loved to chase tail. I figured I could use that to my advantage. Does that make me a bad person? Please don't think I'm a bad person. I could picture Ursula K. LeGuin and Margaret Atwood shaking their heads at me, although I doubt Anais Nin would've had a problem with it.

Side note: As an aspiring Young Adult author I'm obliged to say, stay in school, kids! (And if any kids are reading this, I'm gonna tell your parents. This book is for adults. Older teenagers at the very least. That's a lucrative demo I wouldn't want to miss out on.)

THE PARADOX TWINS
by ALBERT LANGLEY

As soon as we pulled into the parking lot of the nursing home, Max started complaining.

"Do we have to do this?" He checked his precious teeth in the mirror. "You said so yourself, she doesn't even speak most of the time."

"That doesn't mean she won't be happy to see you."

Max pulled a face and parroted the words in a childish sing-song.

That doesn't mean she won't be happy to see you.

"Really, Max?"

I got out of the car and didn't look back. The least he could do while in town was visit Mom once or twice. Get the smallest taste of the responsibility he'd abandoned me with.

To be fair, Mom didn't require a whole lot of effort. I visited once a week (schedule permitting), and it's not like she ever tried to escape or anything. It was the mental burden. The perpetual obligation of it all.

Plus, we'd put her in a top notch facility. As the mother of a famous writer, Mom got treated like royalty. This despite her demeanor. The fact that my brother had funded the Max Langley Memorial Library for Seniors didn't hurt, either. A generous donation that included numerous copies of his complete *oeuvre*. (He claimed the elderly *loved* YA because it made them feel young. I told him the covers would most likely give them seizures.)

Moving on…

Max sprinted to catch up with me. Once inside, an orderly led us into my mother's room. It got a lot of sun and overlooked a pleasant courtyard. Mom sat upright in bed, looking out the window. The walls were bare except for the large wooden crucifix hung over the bed. It looked like something one of my students would have made in remedial woodshop. The orderly tapped his knuckles on the door frame.

"Florence? You have visitors."

She turned to see who it was, then turned back to the window, nonplussed. Despite being in her late 60s, she looked too young to be in an old-age home. An exception to the rule about wearing stress in the face. (*Where* did *she hide her stress*, I wondered. Somewhere a son wouldn't want to see, most likely. A dangling sack of repressed anger under the armpit or nodules of disappointment hidden within her belly folds. Or maybe she'd internalized her negative energy as a teratoma, an amorphous mass of teeth and hair gestating within her.)[21] We entered the room and took our seats.

"Tell 'em to take their shoes off," she said to the window. The window didn't respond. The orderly took the liberty of answering for it as he left.

"You just did, Florence."

---

[21] There are those who believe a teratoma is an underdeveloped or "parasitic" twin, attached to its healthy sibling. Take it a step further and it is a twin that has been partially consumed in the womb by the dominant fetus. Pre-natal sibling rivalry.

I turned to Max. His eyes gave me a last minute plea for reprieve. I shook my head no.

"Did you see who I brought with me, Ma?" I said, still looking at Max. I wanted to enjoy his reaction.

"I seen him."

Max squirmed in his seat. "It's been a long time, Ma."

Mom didn't respond. I made a "keep going" gesture with my hand.

"Uh, how they treating you in this place?"

"You tell me. You're the one paying for it."

God, she was a ball-buster. Maybe it was for the best. Maybe it would make what we'd come to do that much easier.

"Look Ma," I began. "We've got some bad news. It's about Dad…"

"I know all about your father."

Not the response I expected. Had someone told her? We'd given the staff strict orders not to.

"You do?" My throat tightened, trying to choke the words on their way out.

"Came to see me last night. Sat right there where you are now."

She pointed to the chair occupied by Max. He looked down to make sure he hadn't sat on anything. Or anyone.

"Are you sure it was last night?"

"Course I'm sure. He was wearing his good suit, the one he wanted to be buried in."

I exchanged shocked looks with Max.

"Mom, that's not possible… Dad's…"

"Dead?" She shot me an impatient scowl. "I said he was wearing his funeral suit, didn't I?"

I couldn't believe what I'd heard.

"Mom, are you saying Dad came to see you *after* he died?"

She turned her attention back to the window. Back to the courtyard she never bothered going out into.

"He laughed at me for going to church all those years, but he knows the truth now."

Wow. Despite a barrage of follow-up questions, including *Are you trying to tell me Dad's burning in hell?*, we couldn't get any more out of her. Five uncomfortable minutes later Max snuck out without saying goodbye. I got up and put a hand on the cold shoulder mom gave me and said goodnight.

Out in the lobby, I rang for the duty nurse. I found Max leaning against the front desk, back in Max mode.

"Dad must have been super pissed when he found out the afterlife *actually* existed."

"That's not funny."

Mom took her religion seriously. To hear Dad tell it, her piety caused their divorce. Not taking into account all the cheating and boozing he did. And it only got worse after they separated. The piety. (Also, the cheating and boozing. Although I guess if you're separated it's not technically cheating anymore.)

I didn't believe in God, but I took Mom's seriousness seriously. Life couldn't have been easy for a woman of faith living in a house full of scientists. It didn't help matters that they were all men. Dad used to tease her, said if she wanted to topple the patriarchy she should have chosen a less phallocentric belief system, like witchcraft. Comments like that only served to alienate her further.

Things could have been different. I had always wanted to please my mother, and a time existed when I straddled the fine line between faith and facts. But as much as I tried, I never felt that personal connection she always talked about. Never felt any sort of a supernatural presence. People accuse science of being cold and clinical, but my mother's religion suffered from a complete lack of warmth.

I remember the night that sealed my disbelief. My brother and I were sleeping on the floor of my parent's bedroom. We were thirteen or fourteen at the time. A little old to be afraid to sleep alone, but Dad had been on a bender and Mom wanted the company as much as we did. I had waited until Max drifted off to sleep— he could sleep through anything—before voicing my concern.

"Mom? How do you know you're going to heaven?" I asked it in the second person so she'd think I was asking her, personally. Or, you know, for a friend.

At first she didn't say anything. I thought I'd waited too long, that she'd already fallen asleep. But then I heard a sigh. A big one.

Someone let the air out of a tire? Dad's voice in my head.

"You just do," Mom said.

"Oh." Talk about anticlimactic. Like when you were in high school and asked the first kid to lose his virginity what sex felt like, and he replied *awesome*.[22] She was forcing me to put myself out there.

"Sometimes I worry I'm not going to make it."

I don't think she was ready for a philosophical discussion about heaven and hell right at that moment, because her voice rose in pitch and her answer came out more scold than reassurance.

"Don't be ridiculous. Of course you're going to make it."

Glad she felt so confident about it, but that didn't help me any. If the salvation of her family meant that much to her, you'd think she'd draw a fucking map to it like buried treasure. I had a legitimate fear and she failed to address it. It was the last straw as far as religion was concerned.

An overworked nurse rushed into the waiting area. I flagged her down.

"Excuse me, Miss? Do you know if anyone's been to visit my mother in the last few days?"

Her expression said this was not a good time. I doubt a good time existed in her world. She immediately went on the defensive.

"You're the first visitors she's had all week."

"Is there any way at all she could have found out about my father's death?"

She shook her head in an exaggerated manner, and that's when she noticed Max. She went from perfunctory tolerance to sweetness and light.

---

[22] Newsflash: That kid was lying. Young me was something of a habitual liar, so I should know. It brought me no end of trouble growing up, especially in school, although eventually I got better at it.

"Mr. Langley! I didn't know you were here. You should have called ahead."

Max turned on the charm. An involuntary response at this point.

"That's okay… Margaret." He read her name off her name tag. "Just came to see how Mom's doing."

"Oh, she's doing great. Such a pleasure to have her!"

"That's good to hear." Max took a step closer, lowering his voice. "Listen, you don't think there's any way she could have found out about Dad, do you?"

Margaret put a hand on Max's chest. His chest, for Christ's sake!

"I don't see how. She doesn't have a TV and she doesn't read the newspaper. All she does is sit and stare out the window, at that lovely garden you bought for her."

"Thanks, dear." Max slipped a business card into her hand. "I'm only in town a couple of days. Call me."

—

That night the Spaceman visited me again.

My own apartment and the promise of a decent night's sleep were less than a mile away, but I refused to leave Max in the house unsupervised. I physically couldn't do it. My body would revolt if I tried. Somehow override my brain and take control. Did that mean my body had a mind of its own? At least it allowed me to pick up a clean set of sheets on the way back from the nursing home. Small victories, I suppose.

But back to the Spaceman. I had almost drifted off when I felt his presence in the room. It's not like he waltzed through the door—one moment I was alone, the next moment I wasn't. My mother's god could learn a thing or two from that guy. He knew how to make an entrance.

I also felt what I suspect most people would feel if God materialized before them—a lack of control over my bowels. Is that what happened to Dad? Is that where the stains on the mattress came from? They say fear of the unknown is the most irrational of phobias, but this being my second visitation, I can safely say foreknowledge did not make the experience any less scary.

The warmth retreated and the room went cold. If I'd been capable of drawing breath I'm sure I would have seen it when I exhaled. I tried to move but couldn't, once again trapped inside my own body. The shadowy figure stood at the foot of the bed, watching me struggle. I could hear its breathing, heavy with echo. It brought *Blue Velvet* to mind.[23]

Fueled by my fear, the figure began to expand. It grew until it overtook the room, replacing the walls and ceiling with an infinite darkness that stretched out in every direction. A darkness that simultaneously pulled me apart, atom by atom, and crushed me under the weight of its immensity. At that moment I understood the horrors of eternity.

I mustered my strength and pushed against the invisible force holding me down. I pushed against the pins and needles assaulting my body. The cold had caused my

---

23 Millie would have referenced Darth Vader. "*Luke, I am your father…*"

muscles to contract, making every attempted movement a strain, but that didn't stop me. I welcomed the pain. It meant my body still had some fight left in it.

As if sensing my resistance, the darkness tightened its grip. My heart rate slowed. Panic superseded rational thought. I lashed out, thrashing wildly within the prison of my body, pushing against my unseen foe. I pushed and pushed until finally something gave, and I pushed through a state of consciousness, starting awake with a jolt. I looked into the darkness at the foot of my bed.

Nothing.

I got up to get a glass of water. Light floated in from across the house. I could hear Max rummaging around in our father's study. I walked over and casually inquired whether he had been in my room.

"Mom's story getting to you?" I could feel him grinning, even though he had his back to me. It amazed me how quickly he could hone in on the things that bothered me. How much enjoyment he got from picking at them.

"Very funny. What are you still doing up?"

"Looking through some of Dad's old stuff." He held up a stack of white paper. "Did you know he was writing a book?"

I *had* known about Dad's attempt at writing a book. How could I not? When he wasn't complaining it was all he talked about. That being said, he talked about it more than he actually worked on it. A short window existed between buzzed and maudlin in which coherent words flowed, a window which he often missed.

"Book… drunken scribble…" I raise one hand then the other, a human scale weighing the options. Lady Justice sitting in judgment of my father.

"You should have told me. I could have helped."

I laughed in his face.

"There wasn't exactly an open channel of communication. And what makes you think he would have accepted your help?"

"It's a shame." Max leafed through the loose pages. "He led such an interesting life."

Interesting to who? I thought to myself, shaking my head. I left Max to it.

Back in bed, the sheets clung cold and clammy to my skin. Sweat tinged with fear gave off the acrid scent of piss. So much for comfort. I pulled the sheets from the mattress and tossed them to the floor, exposing a now familiar stain. Then I laid down and stared at the foot of the bed, waiting to see what would come for me first—sleep or its dark messenger.

THE THIRD TWIN
by MILLICENT BLACKFORD

I don't know why I felt so nervous about the book signing. Scratch that—I did know, I just didn't want to admit it. It had three letters and rhymed with sax, a word too close to sex to be Freudianly comfortable.

I caught a ride there with Mr. Langley. (I should probably start calling him Alan, to avoid confusion.) He told me the publisher sent a limo, but Max refused to let anyone else ride in it. He didn't want any potential hook-ups to see him arrive with a nerdy brother or pretty girl in tow. Alan's cheeks turned flush when he said the word *pretty*.

Paper and Glue was packed. The event should have been held at one of the chains, but Max wanted to remain loyal to his local independent. Again, for appearances. He sat in a chair behind the podium, next to some of his "people." All smartly dressed types. He seemed energized as he surveyed the crowd of pre-teens, teens, and adults, every once in awhile making a comment to the person next to him. On one such survey his eyes landed on me, prompting a smile. He made a motion with his hand and the next thing I knew a bookseller whisked Alan and I off to a vantage point up by the front.

A pair of posters for Max's latest flanked the podium: *The War For Anthropica*. They depicted the book's retro 70s sci-fi cover. It featured a pair of children in spacesuits leading a charge of psychedelic colors in what looked like an LSD nightmare. Everyone in the audience clutched a copy. A bookseller approached the podium and quieted the crowd. He read from a prepared statement.

"Ten years ago, Max Langley introduced us to Anthropica, a world inhabited by non-humanoid life in a universe completely different from our own. In the sequel, *Children of Anthropica*, he introduced that world to the Earth of the future, an Earth with a dying sun, desperately in need of an alternative form of energy. Despite the incompatibility of the two universes, humans find a way to exploit the Anthropes as a source of fuel. Somehow, in a process I still don't understand the physics of, a pair of Earth children manage to cross over to the Anteverse and attempt to stop its destruction. Now, after years of anticipation, our heroes return in *War for Anthropica*, in which the two universes wage an all out battle for control of the Anteverse. Ladies and gentlemen, I give you the man who made theoretical physics exciting for children of all ages, Mr. Max Langley!"

Max took the podium to rousing applause. He acted more like a movie star than a YA author.

"Thank you, thank you. It's good to be home, back where it all started." This triggered another swell of applause. Max soaked it in, held up a hand with presidential dignity, waiting for the crowd to settle down.

"As many of you know, I came up with the idea for *Anthropica* on the long train ride home after I'd dropped out of college. I was so scared my dad was gonna kick my butt when he found out, I figured I needed something to appease him. When I told him I planned on writing a science fiction novel for young people, he threw me out of the house."[24]

The crowd got a big kick out of that.

---

[24] This isn't entirely true. According to the publisher, Max Langley originally tried to sell *Anthropica* as an adult novel, but they felt it worked better as YA.

"Ten years later I finally put pen to paper and started writing *Anthropica*.[25] Fortunately by then, my brother had decided to become a high school teacher instead of a research analyst at MIT, so that took the heat off me for a while."

Max pointed to Alan and the crowd turned. Alan gave an embarrassed smile. His students made up half the audience. One of them called out, "Yeah, Mr. L!" and everyone laughed. Alan responded with a sheepish wave.

"I wrote the entire book at a bar right here in this town. The owner has been begging me to reveal the location for years, so he can turn the joint into a theme restaurant, but I've sworn him to secrecy. It's too personal a place for me. Of course, he was super pissed when Starbucks sponsored me to write the sequel in coffee shops all over the country, but he's since been compensated."[26]

More laughter.

"This third book, in some ways, has been the most difficult to write. I wrote it in dribs and drabs while traveling the world in support of book two. Despite getting to interact with fans each and every night, a book tour is a lonely endeavor. Still, I can't help but feel blessed. The story is richer for that experience. I incorporated my time in places like South America and India and Russia, places I thought I'd

---

[25] Ten years spent in a drunken stupor, emulating his father. Unlike Millie and myself, who share the sad bond of having no father to emulate.

[26] The location of the actual bar has never been revealed, although a quick Google search provides the internet's generally unanimous consensus. It is an open secret among local residents.

never see except on a map. When the tour ended, I almost didn't want to come home."

Hushed reverence blanketed the crowd. Max looked out over the sea of faces, seemed to look right past them into something intangible beyond. To this day, I still don't know if this was part of the act or genuine sincerity.

"But enough about me[27], it's question time."

A forest of arms shot up. Max pointed one out.

"You, in the purple shirt."

A chubby pre-teen in the second row stood up.

"When is the Anthropica movie gonna come out?"

A couple of the kid's friends tried to get a cheer going, but failed.

"Well," Max said. "The good news is the check cleared." He flashed his famous grin. "But I hear they're having a hard time casting the amorphous molecular beings of the Anteverse."

The crowd laughed. Max was so well rehearsed. They didn't teach you *this* in creative writing class.

"Seriously, though, does anyone think they'll do a good job?"

A chorus of NOs answered the rhetorical question. Max seemed to grow taller as he basked in the attention.

"Who's next? How about the eager beaver in the back?"

Eager Beaver clutched a copy of *War for Anthropica* to his chest.

"Is this really the last book in the series?" he said in a small voice.

---

[27] The tell-tale call of the narcissist. Other characteristics of a narcissistic personality include: egocentric behavior, a sense of entitlement, lack of empathy, chronic lying, and overt criticism.

Max got down on one knee, made direct eye contact with the kid. Made the kid feel like the only person in the room. "Have you finished reading it yet?" Max asked.

The kid gave an enthusiastic nod.

"Who else here has finished the book?" Max returned to his feet, inviting the rest of the crowd to rejoin the conversation. Almost everyone raised their hands.

"Then unfortunately I think you all know the answer to that question."

Sounds of disappointment arose as the crowd deflated.

"So what are you going to do next?" a young mother called out. "You're the only reason my daughter reads."

The kid next to her nodded their head in agreement. A bunch of moms yelled *Yeah!* In solidarity.

"That's a good question, and I'm afraid the answer isn't going to make my publisher very happy." Max looked over at his people. They watched, attentive as the audience. "I've been away from home a long time now, and what with my father's passing, I feel like I've lost my sense of self. No matter how hard he was to live with, my father was a great man and he instilled in me a love of science, and I'll always be grateful for that." He paused to give the moment weight, just the right amount of gravitas before continuing. "Which is why I intend to honor his memory by moving into his house and writing the story of his life."

The audience went dead silent. Not single-corpse dead, but full on mass-grave dead. Only one man survived, and he was standing next to me. Alan's voice shot across the silence like a flare in an apocalyptic wasteland.

"What?!?!"

Then he turned and stormed out of Paper and Glue. Max, ever the performer, held his hand out towards his fleeing brother.

"Albert Langley, ladies and gentlemen."

The crowd offered a smattering of confused applause. Max motioned to the booksellers standing at attention.

"Well, I'm sure everyone's got lots of books for me to sign, so let's start lining people up, and I'll be back in a couple minutes."

Max took off after Alan. I tailed him out the door, processing the spectacle of it all.

—

Alan stalked off across the parking lot, past his car, like he intended on walking the whole way home. Maybe even out of town, into the next state and beyond. Max called after him.

"Albert, c'mon!"

Alan whirled around and retraced his steps, until he stood toe to toe with his brother, finger poking his toned chest.

"You? You're Todd's buyer?"

"He said you wanted to get rid of the place."

Alan started pacing. I held back, watching from behind the cars. I was officially dropping eaves.

"That sneaky fucker!" Alan shouted at the sky.

"Are you mad?" Max softened his tone, trying to calm Alan down. It seemed to work. Alan quit pacing and lowered his voice. He looked more upset than angry.

"You could have at least warned me before announcing it to the whole world."

Max looked around the parking lot of the tiny brick and mortar. I ducked so he wouldn't see me.

"Paper and Glue is hardly the world."

"It's not right. He left the house to me. It's my responsibility."

"And you chose to sell. You've fulfilled your obligation."

Max had a point, and deep down I suspect Alan knew his brother was right. He'd done his part, and the time had come to move on. He seemed about to relent, but then the fire in his eyes returned and he got back in Max's face.

"You had this planned all along, didn't you? That's why you've been snooping around in Dad's stuff. You're capitalizing on his death!"

Max took a step back, put his hands up in the air.

"Whoa! Hold on a second. You really think a memoir about growing up with Dad is what the publisher wants? I nearly gave my agent a heart attack in there."

"Then why are you doing this?"

Alan's voice had returned to peak volume. Max gave him a cushion of silence. He knew how to pace the hell out of an argument. I justified my snooping by telling myself I was witnessing a masterclass in how to write dialogue.

"Don't you wanna know who Dad was?"

"I took care of him for the last ten years. I think I have a pretty good idea."

"Well I don't. I know it's my own fault for leaving, but all I have are memories from childhood, and we both know how easy that was."

Alan pouted.

"It didn't get any easier."

"And here's your chance to find out why. Have you looked at his notes? There's some amazing stuff in there."

"You can't have the house."

Max smiled at this, his teeth solid chunks of charisma.

"You're not gonna make me get a lawyer, are you?"

Alan went silent. He had built up an immunity to his brother's charms, and knew this wasn't an idle threat.

"Mr. Langley?" The name echoed across the parking lot. Both brothers turned to see one of Max's handlers standing in the doorway. I ducked. The handler saw me but said nothing. Max turned back to his brother.

"Look, I gotta get back in there. Can we talk about this later?"

Max knew when he was stonewalled. He beat a hasty retreat while Alan fumed, channeling his anger at the sky. I waited a Max Langley Length Conversation Beat(™) before approaching.

"You okay?"

"I'm fine." Alan seemed less happy to see me each time I popped up. I looked around the parking lot, searching for something to say. I didn't exactly have the most life experience at the time.

"You don't want to share him, do you?"

I thought it sounded pretty astute. Wise beyond my years. I must have come close to the mark, because Alan turned his back to me. I got a quick flash of his father standing in the yard, of the faceless father from my dream. Alan waved his arm in a grand gesture.

"Max can't just swoop in after the fact and pretend like he's been here all along."

I put my hand on Alan's arm.

"Would having your brother around really be that bad?"

More silence followed.

"Do you have any siblings?" he asked. He had me there. I hung my head before answering.

"No."

I don't know why the question made me feel self conscious, but it did. It negated the confidence I felt at my previous insight. I'd give anything to have a sibling, let alone a father to share with them. The grass is always greener, I suppose. Problems are relative. (I know, I know. I couldn't help myself. I don't have a dad, so I've gotta make the dad jokes.)

"It's not easy," Alan said.

"But it's got to be better than not having them, right?"[28]

---

[28] Did you know it is statistically harder for only children to make friends? Siblings prepare one another for social situations outside of the family unit. Without that practice, only children are often awkward and emotionally unequipped for interaction with the wider world. Many never achieve satisfactory integration into polite society.

ANTHROPICA: A CRITICAL ANALYSIS
by Jennifer Tolan

**The Daily Free Press: the independent
student newspaper at Boston University**

Last night saw best-selling author Max Langley appear before a sold out crowd at local bookstore, Paper and Glue. This being Langley's home town, the already accomplished speaker was in exceptional form, and the evening proved quite eventful. During the question and answer session, Langley surprised those in attendance, his publisher, and according to a few attentive witnesses, his own brother, by announcing his next project. Much to the disappointment of his young fans, the book will not take place in the Anthropica universe. Nor will it be a Young Adult novel or even a work of fiction—it will be a memoir about his recently deceased father, noted Massachusetts physicist, Paul Langley.

At this point in his career, Max Langley has earned the clout to do whatever he likes, but the author was not always the publishing juggernaut the public has come to know and love. Written in desperation by a recovering alcoholic surfing friends' couches, the eponymous first book in his Anthropica series saw an initial print run of a mere one thousand copies. Of those thousand copies, credited as being written by Maximilian Langley, approximately fifty are known to exist in saleable condition, fetching upwards of $50,000 each on the collectors market. Despite cribbing much of its premise from sci-fi royalty and recent YA success stories,[29] critics praised Langley's fusion of *bildungsroman* and theoretical physics (although those in the scientific community, including his own father, judged him more harshly), and the themes of family and alienation struck a chord with young readers. There was also a sense of wonderment on display, as illustrated by the novel's opening passage:

Did you ever look up into the night sky and try to count the stars? Think about what life would be like amongst them? Could the planets circling some of those stars be inhabited? What would those beings look like? What if there wasn't just life on other planets, but in other universes? Places where the laws of physics were completely different from our own. Wouldn't you want to go there, if you could?

Mx^2 did.

Strong word of mouth resulted in a slow and steady increase in sales, culminating in an eventual mammoth third printing of one million copies more than a year later. The announcement of a major motion picture deal followed soon thereafter. The rest is history.

---

[29] Max displayed a Tarantino-esque predilection for wearing his influences on his sleeve. From there it is just a hop and a skip to appropriation, pastiche, and yes, even collage. I submit there isn't much difference between what he does and what I am doing. It is just the natural progression of art.

But Langley's cribbage did not go unnoticed by the estates and legal counsel of those who paved the way for him. Words like "influence" and "homage" did not assuage their pockets. No less than three lawsuits had to be settled before the publisher could move forward with a sequel. Because whether Max Langley planned on writing it or not, there was going to be a sequel.

But back to the beginning. The first book in the series consists of two parallel narratives. That of an Earth child named Max (a point the author refused to concede, despite the publisher's insistence), who has recently moved to a new neighborhood and is having trouble fitting in at school. He reads comics and science fiction, and good grades come a little too easy for him. He feels no one understands him, especially his parents, and constantly asks if he was adopted. Pretty standard adolescent angst.

The second narrative revolves around Mx^2, an Anthrope progeny conceived *utero foras*[30] and imprinted with a copy of Max's life energy. The Anthropes use this process to study the mental development of alien races and how they would react to Anthropica's environment, the only way

---

[30] Literally *outside the womb*. Not to be confused with an ectopic pregnancy, in which an embryo attaches itself to the exterior of the uterus, a situation which is generally resolved via chemical or surgical treatment, resulting in termination. In very rare cases ectopic pregnancies have gone unnoticed, resulting in the birth of a healthy child via caesarean. Such was not the case with my mother's third and final attempt to provide me with what would have been a half-sibling.

it would be physically possible due to the fundamental differences between the two universes.

Despite the fact that Max, as the reader knows him, is still a child, the Anthropes are able to imprint Mx^2 with the sum of Max's human experience. This is a result of the way the Anthropes experience time—as a whole as opposed to in increments. The two analogues develop in tandem, feeling both a disconnect from their own lives and a deep connection to an unknown "other."

As their connection grows, the two eventually become aware of each other, and aware that there are hundreds of pairs like them. These cross-dimensional "twins" form a vast network that allows the Anthropes to communicate with Earth. The government of Earth uses this network to exploit the Anthropes in the book's sequel, *Children of Anthropica*, tapping into their very life essence as a source of power. With the third and purportedly final book, *War For Anthropica*, the series morphs from intimate character study into full blown space opera.

Those who wrote think pieces on the liberties taken with the science in the first two books and its detrimental effects on the developing minds of school children will have a field day with *War*, as it seems Langley has abandoned accuracy for story in an attempt to go out with as big a bang as possible. As a writer, it is his right, and in my opinion, the correct choice from a narrative standpoint. Despite the selling point of the Anthropica series being rooted in real scientific principles, it is, after all, a work of fiction. And although bursting at the seams (at nearly 900 pages!) with numerous action set pieces and every plot twist you can imagine, it is still an immensely enjoyable piece of work. One that will delight and frustrate in equal measure.

Will Max Langley be able to maintain his record breaking sales outside the realm of Young Adult Fiction? Most likely not. And both he and the publisher know this. No, Max desires something more ephemeral—literary credibility. The pursuit of which represents the publishing equivalent of a mid-life crisis. He wants to prove he can run with the big dogs. Never mind those dogs are slow and arthritic at this point and cannot hear when their names are called. It is the natural progression of accomplishments. If he scores a critical hit with his memoir, it is another box to tick on the checklist of dreams. If not—oh well, he tried—and it is back to the money-making machine we call YA Fiction.

The following is an excerpt from an early draft of Anthropica, *before the publisher insisted Max tone down the confusing syntax of the Anthrope's communication and target a younger demographic.*

———

As soon as Mx^2 entered the sphere they could feel the protein strands of the progenitors reaching out, attempting to connect. No matter how deep Mx^2 withdrew beneath the surface of the epidermal membrane, it would be impossible to completely block the progenitors out. They would be expecting an explanation as to Mx^2's absence during mandatory information exchange, but Mx^2 required an explanation of their own.

Mx^2 extended a protein strand into the space/time of the sphere. It was encoded in the style of the Earth dialect Mx^2 had absorbed from communion with Max in the Field of Songs. Mx^2 did so knowing full well this would confuse the progenitors, fueling their disapproval.

Progenitors, the information read, *why am I/He the sole satellite existing within the sphere of our unit?* Satellite was the Anthrope analog for child or sibling.[31] Most Anthrope satellites were produced in pairs, each pair sharing a single referential label, or name.

The progenitors took in the strand and absorbed the information. They rejected it almost immediately, as dictated by the rules set forth by the creators of the experiment.

———

[31] Other useful terms, since I am dropping you *in media res* here: Unit = family, sphere = home or domicile. And as you are about to see, the Anthropes don't really do pronouns or prepositions.

(directive) Mx^2 represents applicable referential usage

Mx^2 rearranged the information and resubmitted.

query: subject: additional satellites within unit sphere, correlation: other units (negation) :end query

Mx^2 singular satellite read the reply. It was not an answer to the question. Merely the question regurgitated as a statement.

query: subject: other singular satellites labelled Mx^2 :end query

(negation) additional singular satellites labelled unique referential

query: subject: progenitors referential label (negation) :end query

(positive return) referential label progenitor

Mx^2 understands (negation)

(directive) Mx^2 *exchanges protein strands satellites neighboring units / digestible information recovered*

Mx^2 slipped back into Earth-influenced slang.

I/He am not like the satellites in the other units.

The progenitors scraped the strand clean in frustration, prompting a negative sensory reception from Mx^2.

(priority directive) Mx^2 represents applicable referential usage

Mx^2 gave the Anthrope equivalent of a teenage huff.

Mx^2 compatible satellites neighboring units (negation)

Mx^2 withdrew all protein strands, isolating Mx^2 from the progenitors and the sphere of the unit. Mx^2 then shifted phase to pass through the wall of the sphere into the outer world.

Mx^2 floated among the many spheres of the commune into the barren rock-land beyond. While Anthropes were impervious to the toxic makeup of the atmosphere, they rarely traveled beyond the borders of the commune. Instead they would pass from sphere to sphere, where most of the activities of daily existence occurred. A system of natural caverns existed beneath the commune where social interaction between progeny took place.

In the far reaches of the rock-land, beyond the sight line of the commune, existed the Field of Songs. A series of eddies close enough to Anthropica to be sensed from the surface. The eddies themselves were the warping of space-time by the microscopic matter spheres situated within, but since those spheres were invisible and the Anthropes already used the word sphere to represent domicile, the term eddy stuck. Like Polaris, the Earth's North Star, they maintained a fixed position, and appeared in the sky year round. They funneled background noise said to come from other universes, hence the singing.

A progeny of light enough mass could shift phase and spread its molecules far enough apart to float up into the lower atmosphere to better observe the phenomena. Of course, progenitors attempted to scare them off with horror stories of floating off into space or going mad from the siren song of the eddies. It was there that Mx^2's vague intuitions of a parallel other became strong enough to commune with Max.

Mx^2 knew they should not return so soon after their last visit, but was too agitated to care. It was the only place they felt safe. Mx^2 opened all available receptors to locate transmissions from Max. Despite their many differences, they felt more compatible with Max than any of the satellites from the neighboring units. They even felt more compatible with Max than the members of their own unit. And more than anything else, Mx^2 yearned for the deeper connection only that kind of compatibility could bring. If the progenitors could not provide Mx^2 with such a connection, Mx^2 would take it where they could get it.

The eddies vibrated faster as Mx^2 connected. The volume of the eddies' song increased and Mx^2 got the clearest image yet of what they tapped into. A being of defined shape, one that seemed very impractical. Its epidermal membrane was almost solid, stretched taught to restrict movement. It contained mucous membranes as well as unprotected openings to the outside, but did not seem capable of performing the simple act of phagocytosis to ingest sustenance or allow the exchange of protein strands for communication.

Mx^2 found the creature hideous.

Still, the link felt stronger than ever. This thing understood Mx^2 more than any other satellite in any other unit on any commune. Mx^2 settled in for another long session of information exchange.

If the progenitors continued to deny Mx^2 a complimenting satellite like every other unit in the commune, they couldn't stop Mx^2 from finding one in Max.[32] Most Anthrope life consisted of some type of pair bond—whether between complimentary satellite progeny or progenitor pairs. Denying Mx^2 that bond rendered Mx^2 incomplete—an outcast.

---

[32] Being an only child sucks no matter what planet you live on. And Anthropica ain't the type of place to raise your kids.

When Mx^2 finally reverted form and shifted phase and floated back down, one of the progenitors and a member of the science council awaited. The council member surprised Mx^2 when it extended a protein strand encoded in the vernacular of Earth.

It seems we have a lot to discuss it read.

THE PARADOX TWINS
by ALBERT LANGLEY

The dreaded night finally arrived—Max's triumphant hometown reading at Paper and Glue. I wouldn't have even considered attending if it weren't for Millie. Someone had to keep an eye on her, the right kind of eye, because I knew both of Max's would be.

We arrived to a packed house. I should have realized a good number of my students would be there. They knew better than to bring up Max in the classroom, but here in the outside world they weren't fettered by my gag order. I felt naked, unprotected without it.

Millie and I slipped in late and posted up in the back. Max took to the stage and turned it up to eleven. I couldn't deny it. He excelled at what he did. The crowd hung on his every word, ate out of the palm of his hand—all the clichés applied. And not just the kids and the booksellers, but the adults as well. And the moms—don't get me started on the moms. I would have been mortified if my mother acted the way some of them did.

Such a huge contrast to the first reading Max did back when *Anthropica* came out. Being local he had fancied himself a shoo-in, but Paper and Glue actually turned him down a number of times. Told him adults would come out for an unknown, just for something to do, but the kids, they'd have to be lured in. They had to *want* to go to an event. And for a kid to want to go to an event (especially a book event), there had to be a draw.

Eventually the publisher had to step in, arrange a co-reading with two more well-known YA authors to get Max booked.[33] That made him the opening act. My mother and I sat in the front row. The staff filled in a few seats out of pity. A handful of customers browsing the aisles caught a few phrases here and there, enough to boast about being at Max Langley's first ever book event to their friends years later. When Max opened the floor to questions my mother raised her hand and asked what he wanted her to make for dinner. I don't recall Millie being there. She would have been about fifteen at the time.

Millie. I snapped back to the present. She was eating it up like the rest of them. At that point she hadn't spent enough time with Max for him to lose his shine. I watched her watching him, his words a jumble of white noise in the background. But then one sentence cut through, and it's a sentence I will never forget.

"In honor of my late father's memory, I intend to move into his house, my childhood home, and write the story of his life."

Then all eyes were on me. Had I said something? I closed my mouth. The room shrunk, packing the crowd in tighter, stealing my oxygen. I had to get out of there.

Somehow I wound up in the parking lot, tearing Max a new one. Except I couldn't tear him a new one, because the old one was made of Teflon. Actually, scratch that. He didn't *have* a Teflon asshole, he *was* a Teflon asshole.

---

[33] Both of which Max snubbed once he became successful and it came time to return the favor.

I felt bad for Millie, but I couldn't go back inside after that. I couldn't face the crowd after I'd stormed out like a petulant child. Especially my students. I promised her I'd get Max to sign her books another time and drove her home.

But I wasn't ready to turn in. I had to clear my head. I contemplated asking Millie if she wanted to grab something to eat, but I knew I'd never actually do it. Thinking about acting like a normal human being made me *feel* normal, but if I thought about it too long and it seemed like I might go through with it, I got anxious and killed the idea.

I went to the pub for a beer instead. Not *the* pub, that would have only added insult to ignominy. Especially tonight, when it would be filled with the adult overflow from the reading, and most likely groupies hoping Max would show up. It felt nice to disappear into the crowd, one of the faceless masses who didn't want to be alone but didn't crave human interaction. I stared at the bottles behind the bar and let my eyes go out of focus. The bartender passed by, turned to make sure I wasn't staring at her ass, but once she saw my face she must have realized that ass was the furthest thing from my mind.

—

When I got home I found Max sitting on the couch, looking through a box of old Polaroids. My stomach lurched at the idea of continuing our earlier conversation, but if that was Dad's shit he was going through, I needed to keep an eye on him. So much for my buzz.

"Didn't expect you home so soon," I said.

He didn't look up from the pictures.

"I had to get out of there. Fans can be so cloying sometimes."

At least he hadn't brought a girl home. I panicked for a second, imagining Mille stepping out of the guest room wearing nothing but one of Max's shirts, but then I remembered I had driven her home hours ago. I peeked over his shoulder.

"What're you looking at?"

"Just some old pictures."

No shit, asshat.

Out loud I said, "I thought Mom kept all the photos."

"Not these. Found 'em in Dad's office. Look."

He handed me a stack and I fanned them out like a deck of cards. All intimate shots of nude women with outdated hairstyles, the emulsion faded and warped. I quelled my disgust

"Dad liked his porn old-fashioned. So what?"

Max nudged me. "Keep going."

I flipped through the pile. Somewhere around the middle I came across a smiling picture of our father and an unknown woman, both of them nude. I blanched.

"Oh God."

"Any idea who she is?" Max had obviously seen the picture already, wanted me to discover it organically so I couldn't blame him for thrusting it in my face.

"No." I looked closer. "I'm not even sure this is Dad. I mean, he's smiling."

"You identified the body. Do you recognize his dick?"

I recoiled from the image.

"Don't be crass."

Max picked up a handful of photos and let them fall back into the box. Too many to count.

"I knew Dad had secrets, but…"[34]

We sat there in mutual shock. It was the first sincere moment we'd shared since Max arrived. Even though it was over the discovery of our father's amateur pornography stash, it felt nice.

Okay, maybe nice isn't the right word.

"Listen," Max said. "I'm sorry about the whole thing with the house. I should have come straight to you."

My stomach spasmed again. Who needed crunches with Max around?

"I haven't changed my mind about selling."

"Fair enough."

I stared into the box of pics. I'd rehearsed what I wanted to say to him the whole ride home. The Polaroids only cemented my decision.

"But you were right, about what you said about Dad. I didn't really know him. None of us did. And if you writing that book is gonna help us get to know him better, then I want you to stay here and write that book."

---

[34] A gallery of these Polaroids was featured in the trade paperback version of *Breakfast with the Monolith*. Even though the photos were censored with black bars across the eyes of the anonymous women, it caused quite a stir in the greater Boston area at the time.

MONTAGE:

INT. LANGLEY HOUSE - DAY

Alan walks around the house, filling a garbage bag with trash and empty liquor bottles.

INT. STUDY - DAY

Max pores over his father's mess of notes and papers.

INT. LANGLEY HOUSE - DAY

Alan replaces the photo of the twins on the mantel, in a brand new frame.

EXT. LANGLEY HOUSE - DAY

Alan takes out the trash. He looks up at the Blackford house, sees Millie in her bedroom window, wrapped in a towel, fresh from the shower.

She gently pads the droplets from her chest with another towel. She lifts her arm to run the towel on the skin underneath, exposing the curve of her generous breasts. Is that a nipple we see?[35]

Suddenly, as if she feels the penetrating male gaze upon her, she notices Alan. He quickly averts his eyes.

---

[35] A farcical moment from one of the many terrible screenplay drafts of *BwtM*. There's a whiff of superiority in the screenwriter's mention of the "male gaze," but there's no way that would translate to the screen, what with all the tit rubbing. It's like he's trying to have his gratuitous nudity cake and eat it too. That's the modern male feminist for you.

THE THIRD TWIN
by MILLICENT BLACKFORD

The reading was officially a bust. I'd somehow managed to ingratiate myself even further to the wrong Langley brother. I didn't even get my book signed.

After Alan dropped me off I decided to salvage what little I could from the experience. The next day was critique day in creative writing and I had a story due. I put aside an idea I'd been struggling with—about an alien race so connected to their world they utilized the flora and fauna as additional "senses"—and went with something with a little more verisimilitude.

It poured out of me fully realized: the story of two homeschooled sisters. Their education doubles as an experiment, taking the form of a competition judged by their mother and father. The contest takes place on the world stage via a popular YouTube channel run by the parents. Each week the siblings are assigned a challenge rooted in a different discipline—art, mathematics, physical education, etc. The winner of each week's challenge is awarded basic privileges while the loser is denied. Things like hot food, water, a bed to sleep in. The purpose of the contest is never revealed to the participants, or the reader.

It took less than an hour, my easiest writing session since starting Professor Gable's class. It felt fresh, it had momentum. On top of that, it had something to say.

A jury of my peers tore it to shreds.

Nipple Barbarian[36] helpfully suggested making the story sexier, although he had no notes on how I'd actually go about doing so. Professor Gables called it a surface level satire of fame for the internet generation. Neither commented on what seemed so obvious to me — the complexity of the relationship between the siblings and how the parents exploited that. I thought back to Alan asking me if I had any siblings, a question which, in retrospect, he'd already known the answer to. It'd been a nice way of making a point. *You couldn't possibly understand.* Maybe he was right. Maybe I didn't. I threw the question at the Professor.

"Do you have any siblings, Professor Gables?"

He didn't miss a beat.

"Yes, three."

"What about you?" I asked the only other woman present in class. I'd caught her off guard.

"I, well… I have a brother, but… we get along great."

I narrowed my eyes at her, the word TRAITOR flashing red in my mind. She apologized with a sheepish shrug.

"Fine." I crumpled my paper into a compact display of anger and fired it at the waste basket. I missed, which only made me angrier. I turned back to Nipple Barbarian. "Would you have enjoyed the story more if I hadn't worn a bra today?" He gave the idea more consideration than anything I'd said all semester. The Professor, to his credit, maintained

---

[36] Little known fact: Nipple Barbarian, AKA Howard Roberts, went on to create the popular fantasy comic, *The Erotic Adventures of Carbor*. Go figure. He's actually a really nice guy. Misunderstood, as many nice guys are.

eye contact, his mouth a perfect horizontal line. He let the dust from that skirmish settle before moving on.

"Anyone else have any thoughts?"

I knew I wouldn't be getting anything constructive from the class for the rest of the semester. I grabbed my bag and stormed out. On my way, I noticed the quiet guy who sat in the back had picked up my crumpled story and smoothed it out.[37] At least someone had appreciated it.

---

[37] Despite sounding like *The Truman Show* meets *Dogtooth* (the latter obviously influenced by the Mexican film *The Castle of Purity*—yet again proving there is nothing new under the sun, just innumerable variations), I'd love to get my hands on that story, if it still exists. Work the text into this narrative. Plus, it would make quite the collector's item. Quiet guy in the back of class, if you're reading this, get in touch!

"SIBLING RIVALRY"
by MILLIE BLACKFORD[38]

Like many of you, I have a vivid memory of the first time I saw *Sibling Rivalry*. A friend of mine had insisted I watch it. "You're not going to believe this," she told me. "You thought your parents were bad…"

She sat me and my low expectations in front of the computer and clicked play on the first webisode in the series. A shrill bell sounded, introducing the contestants: Sisters, a year or two apart, named Maxine and Alice. They sat wide-eyed and at-the-ready, in a homeschool environment that came off more dungeon than classroom. Their first challenge: to write a personal essay. "What I Did On My Summer Vacation." Being best friends who spent every waking hour together, the results read blandly similar. Sunny days spent exploring and napping and swimming in the pool. Maxine won, but barely. The decision seemed almost arbitrary. Her reward was dinner, and not sleeping on the floor of the garage *cum* classroom.

The post-challenge interviews presented little conflict, coming off as vanilla as the essays that preceded them. Both girls bubbled with excitement on screen.

---

[38] Quiet Guy comes through! Thank you for your help, kind stranger!

Also, I took the liberty of naming the previously unnamed sisters. It makes the story easier to follow and I couldn't resist the thematic implications.

Me-and-my-sister this, *me-and-my-sister* that. Even Alice, who lost the inaugural challenge. She equated sleeping in the garage to camping. A novelty. Something fun.

But that didn't last long. Challenge #2 was a physical one. A mile-long obstacle course in the park. A small crowd gathered as the girls jogged from station to station, performing a different exercise at each. Bipartisan cheers urged them on. Their parents watched intently, making notes and keeping time. After losing this challenge as well, Alice, worn out from the exertion, could not muster any enthusiasm for spending a second night on the garage floor. Especially without a hot meal or shower. A bottle of water and a single slice of Wonder Bread did little to comfort her. When she got up in the middle of the night to use the bathroom, she found herself locked out of the house proper. She held it in as long as she could before peeing in the corner by the rakes.

Meanwhile, her sister fell asleep with a full belly in a warm bed. In the post challenge interviews, conducted the following morning, Maxine arose refreshed and chipper, although to her credit she did express concern for her defeated sibling. She floated the possibility of letting Alice win one, sharing the burden so her sister didn't have to endure all the unpleasantness. The parents had anticipated, even hoped for this, and the prospect made them giddy. It ticked off boxes on the checklist of their experiment.

The next challenge was one of mathematical prowess. The parents considered both girls certified math whizzes.

They often recited multiplication tables to each other for fun. So it only took a couple simple "mistakes" for Maxine to lose. She took the loss with dignity and grace, and Alice—senses dulled from two nights spent in the garage—was none the wiser. Alice enjoyed a fortifying meal, a hot bath, and a good night's sleep.

Maxine, however, expecting a prisoner's meal and a night in the garage, received a different punishment—a night in the backyard without food or blanket. Not bad, considering she could pee in the bushes if necessary. Maxine waved to Alice, who watched from their bedroom window, confident she had done the right thing. Alice put her hand against the glass in solidarity. Then she fell right asleep with only a tiny twinge of guilt.

Maxine settled in for a long night. She nodded off, sleeping in fits and starts. The grass proved comfortable enough, but damp grass made for chilly bones. At one point she awoke to a rustling in the dark and the pungent scent of decay. She sat up and put a hand over her nose, strained her ears to decipher the sound. Startled at her movement, something jumped back. Maxine pulled her knees to her heaving chest. Something ripe covered her pants. She retched, attempted to wipe her arms off on the grass. As she did she felt tiny hands grasping, pawing at her feet.

She screamed.

The backyard lights flashed on, illuminating a mother raccoon and three babies, attempting to feast on the garbage smeared across her legs. She kicked and continued to scream, causing the hungry animals to scamper off into the night.

She ran for the back door but found it locked. She pounded on the glass, screaming to be let in, but no one came. She stepped back and looked up, towards the kitchen window. Her parents watched from within the shadows of the house, but made no move to help. She beat the door until her hands got sore. Her energy expended, she slid to the ground and cried. The lights clicked back off.

Maxine was unable to sleep the rest of the night, yet found herself startled awake when her father turned the hose on her the next morning. Her post-challenge interview came out a garbled mess of half sentences and whimpered pleas.

Alice already sat at one of two school desks when their father ushered Maxine into the garage. Alice's eyes expanded as Maxine sat next to her, shivering and soaking wet.

"What happened?" Alice whispered to her sister.

"No talking!" her father barked in response.

Maxine fixed her sister with a stare. It contained no malice. Only resolve.

There were no more intentional losses after that. From that moment on, both sisters played to win. It became a matter of survival, because as the competition went on, the punishments continued to get worse. A night spent locked in a cage. Being driven to an undisclosed location and forced to walk home. A night spent naked in the trunk of a car, on a busy street in a bad neighborhood. Never any food, never any amenities.

There was no more concern expressed in the post-challenge interviews. No more kind waves through bedroom windows, and certainly no conversing in the classroom. There were taunts, and sabotage, and death stares. Sometimes the little boy next door watched, perplexed. Was this what it was like to have a brother or sister?

Rabid fandoms cropped up around each sister. Team Maxine. Team Alice. Official merchandise did a brisk business (bootleg even more so). Podcasts and live blog streams crunched numbers, studied every angle, and made predictions. Social media arguments went for the jugular. Vegas bookers assigned odds and accepted bets. Reports even showed up on mainstream media outlets. Crowds armed with hand-written signs posted up outside of local morning shows, and fans bombed on-location reporters. *Sibling Rivalry* became a full blown phenomena.

The challenges became more elaborate and the punishments more creative, thus the show became less realistic. This supported the opinion of those who insisted the whole thing was scripted, a hoax. Still, pearl-clutching media watchdogs denounced the show, calling for the heads of the parents or whatever entity subjected children to such abuse in the name of entertainment. But as no one knew where the show originated (although the FBI was on the case), all anyone could do was watch.

And watch they did. The world held its collective breath going into the final challenge—a boxing match between the two sisters. In terms of the competition they were neck and neck. The winner of said match would be declared champion, and reign under the title of "Daughter of the Year." In terms of the experiment, their parents seemed beyond ecstatic. They constantly whispered behind their clipboards, making notes and observations, patting each other on the back. Both Maxine and Alice appeared weak due to stress and the back and forth of the physical punishment. A single night in a warm bed did nothing at that point. Full recovery would require much more time.

Despite this both girls fought like abused animals. Swinging and kicking and spitting and biting. Arms and legs and saliva and teeth. Within seconds they had wrestled one another to the ground. Neither parent stepped in to referee. The three minutes between bells seemed an eternity, played out in real time to maximize the violence. Each blow landed caused me to wince, as if I watched myself fighting inside the ring. Off in the distance I could hear my neighbors calling for blood.

Eventually both girls collapsed from exhaustion. They didn't even make it three rounds. Clothes were torn and eyes bruised black. Blood spattered the concrete floor of the garage as they lay heaving. The parents retreated to a corner to tally the score. Shots landed. Effective aggression. Ring generalship. The Ten-point Must System.

The sisters crawled back to their respective corners and waited. No hugs or bumped fists or even nods. No sportsmanlike expression of a fight well fought. When their parents stood them next to each other for the decision, there was no eye contact. Only grit teeth and clenched muscles. Tight, unbalanced sways. The parents played the moment for all it was worth. When they declared the fight a draw, both girls burst into tears.

Most people took to social media to register their disgust. News outlets reported scattered rioting in the real world. It made great water cooler conversation the next day. A week later people had already stopped talking about it.

In the final post challenge interviews, conducted after they'd recovered a bit, neither Maxine nor Alice discussed the outcome of the fight, or the competition as a whole. Instead they talked about the upcoming winter break, and what they'd be doing with their time off. Their plans involved plenty of rest and holiday family fun. Cocoa and carols. Hopefully there'd be snow. The girls seemed normal, smiles stretched taut as they spoke, but something felt off. Their eyes stared past the camera, at a distant point the viewer couldn't see. It became the subject of much online discussion, but I understood almost immediately. As much as I'd grown to love these two sisters and didn't want to see them hurt, I couldn't help but feel disappointed at the outcome of the competition. The lack of a clear winner. And the look in their eyes told me they felt the same exact way.

THE PARADOX TWINS
by ALBERT LANGLEY

We spent the next few days cleaning up the place. Well, I did most of the actual cleaning, but Max sorted through Dad's disaster of an office, which I didn't have the patience for. It felt nice. Two brothers working together towards a mutual goal. We didn't talk much, but we didn't fight either, so… baby steps.

We started at opposite sides of the house and by the end of the second day we'd met in the *de facto* middle—Dad's bedroom. Max joined the task already in progress, perusing yet another pile of books while I went through the closet.

"Want to see something weird?" I stood aside to reveal a row of identical Khaki pants and white button-down shirts, pressed and hung. An odd display of order at the center of a maelstrom of disarray. Max looked up from the book he leafed through, some outdated physics text.

"Just like his hero."

His hero, my namesake.[39]

I tried to remember what Dad wore the last time I saw him, but could only conjure up his disapproving face. A mental fog obfuscated anything below the neck.

"I thought the whole thing about Einstein wearing the same clothes every day was a myth," Max said. "Didn't his wife insist on keeping him in fancy dress?"

---

[39] Another way in which Paul Langley resembled his hero—both were inveterate ladies' men. In a series of letters released to the public in 2006, it was revealed Einstein's philandering ways were no secret to his family, and he took pleasure in regaling his wife and step-daughter with his sexual exploits abroad.

I willed Max to shut up for a second, so I could concentrate on this one slippery detail that suddenly seemed so important. The clothes make the man, and all that, but it had been years since Dad had given a shit about outward appearances. And I doubt he'd ever picked up an iron his entire life.

"That was his second wife," I heard myself answer as I struggled to focus. "Who I believe was his cousin."

Max nodded his head, as if the motion somehow activated the mechanism in his mind that processed information.

"Maybe that's why Dad never re-married."

I gave up. The image of Dad's stern face dissipated.

"He was too set in his ways?" I said.

"No, he didn't have any cousins."

Max seemed plenty pleased with that little *bon mot* as he went back to his books. I disappeared back into the closet, resumed rooting around. Dad didn't have much in the way of footwear, but made up for it by saving piles of old magazines secured with twine. In the darkest corner I found a box of VHS tapes. I picked one up and steeled myself for more porn. The rare pleasant Dad-related surprise awaited me.

"Hey, look at this," I said from within the confines of the closet.

"Sorry, can't hear you from all the way over there in Narnia."

I crawled back out and tossed the tape to Max. An old home video copy of Stanley Kubrick's *2001: A Space Odyssey*. Dad's favorite movie.

It ain't a movie, it's a film Dad corrected me. *A piece of art!*

Dad had tried to indoctrinate us into the church of Kubrick before we'd even had the attention span to sit through a Disney film. Years later, when he would pass out drunk in front of the television, Max and I would crawl into the living room military style and flank the recliner to watch as apes bashed each others brains in and a computer committed the very human act of premeditated murder.

"Is this *the* copy?" A simian spark appeared in Max's eyes. "I'll fight you for it."

Dad would have loved that. The two of us, grown men, rolling around on the floor for a scrap from his table, some sort of posthumous trophy.

"Take it," I told him. "I always liked the book better."

"Another reason I can't believe we're brothers."

Max couldn't take his eyes off the faded cover. It was the original 1980 VHS release. The silver one, with the painting of Space Station V, a rocket shooting out of its docking bay.

"Thanks, Al. This means a lot."

I smiled. My brother rarely expressed genuine gratitude. He ran a thumb against the worn edges of the cover.

"He must have watched this a thousand times," Max said. "Think it still works?"

Never in a hundred years would I have predicted we'd end that night sitting in our father's house watching *2001* together. We'd now bonded twice over the bastard in as many days. And this time because of an honest-to-goodness pleasant memory, not some shared awkwardness. We flanked the recliner, like in the old days (although we sat cross-legged, as the idea of two grown men lying on their stomachs, chins in their hands and feet in the air didn't seem dignified). Every once in a while I'd glance up at the empty recliner, half expecting to see Dad's silhouette in the glare of the TV. As Dave Bowman jogged the centrifuge at the heart of the *Discovery*, I thought, *It's good to be home.*

The feeling didn't last long, though. Millie showed up with some food Mrs. Blackford had made and before I knew it I was playing second fiddle to the charm monster yet again. I tell you, Max knew how to burn through some good will. Made me glad I hadn't told him that every other tape in Dad's closet had been porn of the "barely legal" variety. Ugh. I made a mental note to bag them up and get rid of them under the cover of night.

Until then I had to stand there and watch as Max channeled Dad in a peacock-like display of braggadocio. Just like in the fucking old days. He brought up personal details I would have preferred to share with Millie in private, if the occasion ever presented itself. Instead he used them to undercut me at every opportunity. The specifics aren't germane to the story as a whole, so you'll forgive me for moving on out of fear of being redundant.[40]

---

[40] Kind of a cop out, but no matter. Millie included a *very* specific account in *The Third Twin.*

This is a total pet peeve of mine. Fear is one of the biggest detriments there is to real, honest writing. And more often than not, writers that attempt to hide the truth from their readers will leave behind clues, whether unintentionally or out of a subconscious desire to make that truth known. *Always* be honest with your readers, as I have always been with you, dear friends.

THE THIRD TWIN
by MILLICENT BLACKFORD

I shifted the aluminum tray to my left hand and used the right to smooth down my blouse. Mom had given me a strange look when I told her I needed to change before I brought her care package over to the Langleys, but she didn't say anything. That was generally her way. Show don't tell. It made her cues easier to ignore. Unless we were standing face to face during the transfer of a tray full of pasta. That made it impossible. Still, I managed to make it out of the house with minimal reproach. After standing on the Langley's porch a few minutes wondering whether they were home or not I realized I hadn't knocked yet.

Alan answered the door. He seemed surprised to see me, but then, he always seemed surprised to see me. Deer in the headlights surprised.

"Oh, hi Millie…" His surprise bordered on embarrassment. Being an especially empathetic person, it made *me* feel embarrassed. My leg started twitching.

"Hey, Alan."

Right before I could launch into my spiel, he decided to kick the awkwardness up a notch.

"Sorry about earlier. I…"

Earlier. Right. Why am I even including this? In my initial draft I made a note for my future agent, telling *them* to tell *me* to cut this bit. Eventually, when I secured said agent, they told me that when it comes to memoir, warts and all is the way to go. And I had way more unsightly warts than this, so…

I guess I should explain. Earlier in the day, Alan and I had made awkward eye contact through my bedroom window after I had just gotten out of the shower. Having just gotten out of the shower, I wore nothing but a bath towel. I mean, at the most he saw some top shoulder, but still...

I immediately cut him off at the pass.

"Don't worry about it. Mom always yells at me for walking around the house in a towel." Why would he even bring that up? It's the unspoken law of neighbors: if you catch your neighbor in a less than flattering position, YOU DO NOT BRING IT UP. I needed a segue, and fast.[41]

"Speaking of Mom..." I held up the tray. "She made lasagna." I handed off the care package. We both stood there smiling like dummies. "Can I come in?"

Look at the big balls on Millie.

"Oh yeah, sure. Come on in."

I followed him into the house, which looked substantially cleaner than the last time I'd seen it, which had been when Mr. Langley — the original Mr. Langley — had still been alive. Better not to bring it up.

"Don't mind the mess," he said. "I'm still going through Dad's things."

So much for that. Better him than me, I guess. That's when you-know-who poked his head out from behind the recliner.

"We have guests?"

My heart jumped. I tried to tell myself Max had startled me.

"It's Millie," Alan said. "Mrs. Blackford sent over some food."

---

[41] So naïve. It is a quality in Millie I miss. These days, she takes her privacy much more seriously. One of the tradeoffs of success, I suppose.

"Excellent. I'm starved." Max smiled and jumped to his feet. I couldn't tell if he smiled for the lasagna or for me.

I followed Alan into the kitchen, where I went on auto-pilot and unwrapped the pasta. He went about business in his usual shell-shocked manner, but Max jumped right in and grabbed some plates and silverware. I started doling out portions.

My mother called pasta The Great Equalizer.[42] Put a disparate group of people around a table, serve them pasta, and watch a family atmosphere evolve. It didn't matter who they were.

And I have to admit, her theory held gravy. At first the three of us ate in silence, but by the time we finished, the mood in the room had become more relaxed. Even Alan seemed less on edge.

"This tastes excellent," Max said, mouth full, pointing at his plate with his fork.

"Glad you like it. Mom still thinks of you guys as the boys next door."

Such a thought had probably never crossed mom's mind, but it kept the conversation rolling.

"Nothing wrong with that," Max said as he shoveled it in. Alan took small, sensible bites. They were so different. I found it hard to believe they were even related. My curiosity exceeded my manners.

"So let me ask you something. If you guys are identical twins, how come you look nothing alike?"

---

[42] My mother called it poor people food, unironically, despite our own economic status.

Alan looked down at his plate. Shit, maybe the equalizing effects of the pasta worked *too* well. I shouldn't have been so familiar. But Max grinned.

"Albert and I were discussing that just the other day, weren't we, Al?" He turned his penetrating gaze on Alan. Alan continued to stare into his plate, pushing food around with his fork.

"Don't call me Albert."

"We couldn't seem to come to a consensus." Max continued to bore eye-holes into his brother. "Al rejected my lifestyle hypothesis."

Alan worked up the defiance to meet his brother's gaze.

"Is stuffing your big mouth with lasagna part of your 'lifestyle' now?"

Max bounced a slap off his tight abs. It echoed across the house.

"It's called a cheat day."

Time to go into damage control. I said the first thing that came to mind.

"Maybe if you separate twins for too long they begin to lose their twinness."

God, it sounded stupid. Paging my impending adulthood. Where the hell are you?

"Actually, that might not be so far from the truth," Max said. "Have you ever heard of the Twins Paradox?"

"Oh, jeez…" Alan rolled his eyes.

"See? Albert knows what I'm talking about."

Consider my interest piqued. I was torn between easing the tension and finding out more.

"I'll bite. What's the Twins Paradox?"

Alan interjected. "An allegory our father used to pit us against one another."

Max stayed him with a hand.

"Albert, please." He turned back to me. "The Twins Paradox, Millie, is a thought experiment in special relativity in which one twin takes a near light speed journey in a rocket ship and returns to find he has aged less than the twin who stayed behind on earth."

I tried to gauge his level of seriousness.

"So that's where you've been all these years? On a cosmic voyage?"

"Not literally, but I am out of this world."

Would you like to swing on a star...

Max grinned at his own cheesy joke. A good three seconds passed before I burst out laughing.

"I'm sorry," I told him. "That was awful."

Alan threw his hands in the air.

"And now you see my father's power to instigate competition from beyond the grave."

"I don't know," I said. "It kinda works as a theoretical explanation for sibling rivalry."

Max elbowed his brother in the ribs, none too gently.

"See? She gets it."

"What it *doesn't* explain," Alan went on to say, "is why the brother in the rocket ship acts like such a dick."

I laughed so hard a piece of lasagna got caught in my throat, prompting a coughing jag. This time, it was Alan's turn to grin.

THE PARADOX TWINS   111

"Laugh it up, you two," Max said as he waited for the giggles to subside. He knew when he'd been got.

The lasagna must have really done the trick, because next thing I knew I heard myself suggesting we all go out for a beer, like old friends. Alan reverted back to his usual self, shaking his head no, saying he didn't think it was a good idea. So I started second guessing myself, thinking maybe I'd crossed another line, and adding alcohol to the situation would make things even weirder, but then Max cut the thought off by saying he knew just the place. I looked over at Alan again, hoping he'd change his mind, because I wasn't one hundred percent comfortable being alone with Max.

"Well, maybe just a quick one..."

Yes! Operation *Ingratiate Myself with a Famous Author* was in full effect.

We piled into Alan's car. Max followed his brother around to the driver side and pushed him over to the passenger seat.

"I'm driving."

Alan grudgingly complied.

"I know how to get there," he said.

"Yeah, but you can't shake a tail to save your life."

Alan huffed like an incredulous nobleman, an amazing sight to behold."You're not *that* famous," he said. "No one's following you."

Max grinned for the hundred forty-seventh time that evening. He turned the key in the ignition.

"You'd be surprised."More huffing from Alan. I poked my head over the front seat.

"So where are we going?"

I have to admit, I had a buzz going, and we hadn't even started drinking yet. Max put his hand against my forehead and pushed. A gesture that could be considered either intimate or condescending. I gave him the benefit of the doubt.

"Sit back and be quiet," he said. "Don't make me blindfold you."

"Oh, secretive. I'll play." This definitely felt intimate. I put my hands over my eyes.

"Don't encourage him," I heard Alan say.

But I was having too much fun. I felt the car lurch into gear and roll out. When I finally took my hands away from my eyes, after Alan had helped me from the car and led me by the elbow, we were standing in a dark alley in front of a padlocked door. Max produced a key and held it up for all (two of us) to see. I swear it twinkled in the night, like he'd sprinkled it with magic fairy dust.

"You're kidding," I said. "You have your own private entrance?"

Max grinned and jiggled the key into place. It fit but wouldn't turn. He rattled the lock harder. His smile faded as ours grew.

"Looks like your old lady changed the locks on you," I said.

Cut to us walking through the front door like a couple of regular jerks. Max gave the obvious appearance of someone attempting to keep a low profile, but only a solitary middle-aged waitress recognized him. Her dead eyes came back to life when she saw him.

"Long time no see, sugar!"

She sidled up and Max gripped her by the shoulders and planted a kiss on her cheek, accompanied by an exaggerated onomatopoeia.

"Mwah!"

"You want the usual?" She traced the corner of her mouth with a pinkie finger, to make sure her lipstick hadn't smudged.

"Yes ma'am."

"Tonic water, twist of lime." She winked as she said it. Shot him the finger-gun. I blanched at the wink and beverage both.

"Ew?"

Max ignored my disgust.

"And whatever my guests desire."

How magnanimous. Alan and I each ordered a beer and Max herded us to a booth in the back corner. It all started to make sense.

"So this is where the famous Max Langley wrote his very first book," I said.

"How astute." He gave my arm a playful touch. "It's also where I had my very last drink."

This pissed off an already pissy Alan even more.

"It's also the bar where our father drank himself stupid every night."

The remark earned him a slap in the arm from his brother. A backhand. Playful, yet firm.

"Come on, Albert, is that really necessary?"

"Don't call me Albert." Alan massaged his stinging tricep.

"I'm sorry," I interrupted. "I didn't mean to get personal."

"That's alright." Max shot Alan a look. "Some of us take things more personally than others." I decided to change the subject to one of Max's favorites — himself.

"So how did a children's book based on theoretical physics become an international best-seller?"

"Kids are smarter than we give them credit for." Max's reply sounded well rehearsed.

"Please," Alan said. "The average high school student doesn't understand the underlying principles Max based the books on." His defense against his brother's competitive nature took the form of a wall of belligerence. I poked him in the ribs and he jumped a good six inches.

"So explain them, smarty pants."

Alan narrowed his eyes into accusatory slits.

"I thought you found science boring?"

He had me there. Right as I had started to feel like one of the adults, too.

"Science *class*. This is different."

"I don't know…" Max said. "This might be a little over Albert's head…"

"…says the man who dropped out of college," Alan finished for him.

"Says the man who wrote 'the book that changed the way we look at physics.'" Max punctuated the sentence with air quotes before turning to me. "My publicist wrote that."

"She's good," I told him. Our faces hovered so close I could smell the not-so-unpleasant scent of tonic water and lime. Did tonic have a scent? I know it tasted bitter, but what did bitter smell like?[43]

"Fine!" Alan mini-exploded. It seemed he did not appreciate our facial proximity. "You want it explained? I'll explain. Certain fundamental constants exist that shape the physics of our universe. Speed of light, mass of an electron — that sort of thing. Previous thought suggested you couldn't tamper with those values without making life as we know it impossible. But recent experiments have shown that as long as you have elements congenial to carbon based life, you could alter the masses of the elementary particles. Thus — the entities of The Anteverse. The difference in the nuclear force accounts for their physicality. The rest he ripped off of Isaac Asimov and J.K. Rowling,[44] and doesn't require any knowledge of actual science."

Alan finished his tirade-slash-lecture to stunned silence. It was Max's turn to look annoyed. I have to admit, Alan had impressed me. I was *this* close to initiating a slow clap.

---

[43] Tonic water's bitter taste can be attributed to the alkaloid *quinine*, which is derived from the bark of the *cinchona* tree. Its main use is as an antimalarial drug, but it can also be used to treat restless leg syndrome, an affliction Millie has been known to exhibit when nervous. It's the reason she brings a floor-length table cloth to all of her book signings.

[44] *Anthropica* owes a huge debt to Asimov's *The Gods Themselves*. I'd add Dan Simmons' Hyperion Cantos to that list as well.

BREAKFAST WITH THE MONOLITH
- JAGER CARTWRIGHT - 7/9/15 DRAFT

EXT. LANGLEY HOUSE - NIGHT

Alan, Max and Millie approach the
stoop. There is obvious chemistry
between Max and Millie as they chat.

> ALAN
> (interrupting)
> It's getting kind of late…

Max and Millie make no move to go.
Alan stands there in awkward silence
as they continue to talk. Finally,
Millie notices.

> MILLIE
> You know what? I think I'm gonna
> head home. I had a great time,
> guys. Thanks for the science
> lesson.

> MAX
> Goodnight, Millie.

> MILLIE
> Goodnight.

INT. LANGLEY HOUSE - SAME

Alan slams the door behind him.

> ALAN
> What the hell do you think you're
> doing?

> MAX
> What's your problem?

> ALAN
> She's our neighbor's daughter.
> She's only nineteen, for Christ's
> sake!

> MAX
> I see what this is about. You're
> jealous.

> ALAN
> Oh, grow up. You sound like one
> of my students.

> MAX
> Hey, you don't have to explain it
> to me. I get it. I come across
> dozens of Millies at book events
> all over the country.

                    ALAN
So then you'll have no problem
leaving this one alone.

                    MAX
Alright, man, no sweat. She's all
yours.

                    ALAN
It's not like that.

                    MAX
Whatever you say, Humbert. I'll
keep my distance.[45]

---

[45] Why did I choose to include this little throwaway exchange from the screenplay? In light of Millie's comment about her creative writing professor "forcing Nabokov down the supple throats" of female students, I thought it thematically appropriate. The screenwriter must be a big fan of Millie's memoir.

THE PARADOX TWINS
by ALBERT LANGLEY

My life spiraled out of control, like matter in an accretion disc moving towards the central body. The time had come for drastic measures. So the next day I did something I hadn't done in almost ten years—I exercised. A mile and a half of nauseous huffing in full view of the entire neighborhood. Not that they cared or paid any attention, but I felt so out of shape and out of place I imagined their derisive stares peeking out from behind their shades as I passed. Sweat dripped from the baseball cap I had pulled low over my eyes to hide my identity.

This after I had done something else I hadn't done in years—gotten a physical. The person who answered the phone at the doctor's office didn't understand why I needed an appointment that day, but luckily they had an opening and obliged me. I had spent the night before doing damage control, sucking in my gut and pinching pudge in the mirror. I anticipated the worst. Maybe even the C word. There had to be an explanation other than the Twins Paradox.

I sat on the exam table buttoning my shirt, waiting for the inevitable bad news. As humiliating as all the poking and prodding seemed, the doctor's post-exam chastisement always felt worse.

"Your cholesterol's a bit high and you could stand to lose a few pounds," the doctor told me, "but other than that, you're in decent shape."

That was it? No death sentence? I contemplated getting a second opinion.

"Well then how do you explain my brother?"

"I really couldn't say without examining him." The doctor put aside his clipboard. "There have been numerous studies about twins and aging,[46] most of which focus on lifestyle choice, not separation."

Great. I didn't like where this was going.

"So what you're telling me is I've got to be more like my brother to be more like my brother."

"As far as the physical. Otherwise, I'd wager you're more alike than you think. Even twins who've never met have very similar personalities."

I laughed out loud. It could have been classified as a guffaw.

"They even wind up with similar wives because they have the same inherent taste in women."

"Yeah, well… my brother's not the marrying type." I looked down at my fat rolls.

"And you are?"

Cut to me lumbering down the sidewalk in my sweats.

Max had managed to drag himself out of bed by the time I'd finished my run. We converged in the kitchen for water and coffee. I opened the refrigerator door in an attempt to place a barrier between us, to hide my clothes, anything to deflect attention. I felt the confrontation coming in three… two… one…

---

[46] One of the most famous, as close to testing the Twins Paradox as we've come yet: in 2015/2016, astronaut Scott Kelly spent a year in space while his identical twin brother, Mark, got the boring job of staying on Earth as the control.

"Since when do you jog?" His smug tone belied the innocence of the question. I sighed from inside the refrigerator.

"The doctor said I could stand to lose a few pounds."

I pictured Max grinning, the arrogant fuck.

"I could have told you that. In fact, I'm pretty sure I already did."

I popped my head out of the fridge.

"I wanted a second opinion."

"I see…" Max scratched at the stubble on his neck while I reached for a bottle of water.

"This wouldn't have anything to do with a certain young lady who lives next door, would it?"

I hit my head against the top of the refrigerator. Pain fueled my anger.

"What did I tell you about that?" I slammed the refrigerator door and pointed the bottle at his chest. Max took a step back, hands raised in mock surrender.

"Hey, plenty of people get in shape to further their platonic relationship with the hot twenty-something next door. It's totally normal."

I was fighting a losing battle, so I changed the subject. The only thing Max enjoyed more than harassing me was talking about himself.

"How's the research going?"

"Don't think I don't see what you're trying to do, but it's going great. Our father was a strange and fascinating man. Did you know he freelanced at NASA?"

I hadn't. Or at least I didn't think I had at the time.

—

That night the Spaceman finally stepped out of the darkness and revealed himself to me. Had my brother's words given form to my fear? All I know is, once I named my late night visitor, he (it?) retroactively became the Spaceman in all my previous memories. Even ones from my childhood, because, holy shit— had he been visiting me my whole life? Had I suppressed the memories? The thought chilled my insides. I pictured him standing over me in my crib as I wailed for my mother. There he was, watching from the doorway while eight-year-old me cowered under the covers, wetting the bed out of fear instead of getting up to use the bathroom. His vast darkness permeated my teens, echoing back my own insecurities while I lay awake at night. My brother and I shared a room our whole childhood, how had Max never seen him?

But I'm getting ahead of myself. That visit started out the same as all the others. A shadowy figure materialized at the foot of the bed, watching as I struggled against my paralysis. I ignored the pins and needles that assaulted my body. If only I could move, I'd reach out and grab the darkness, confront it. If I fell into it and disintegrated, so be it. At least I would know I had tried. So I pushed. I pushed so hard my muscles seized. I pushed and I pushed until finally it felt like something gave and I tore free. But right as my body sprang forward, the mattress beneath me disappeared. I fell from a great height, splashing down into a lake of cold sweat.

I started awake and stared into the darkness. Were my eyes playing tricks on me or did I see the outline of a person?

"Max? Is that you?"

I got no response. I tried not to, but couldn't help flashing back to Max's innocuous question about NASA, his comments about Mom's post funeral "visits" from our father. This was just my subconscious freaking me out, right?

"Dad?" I whispered it, hoping the presence wouldn't hear, wouldn't respond. I held my breath and listened. I leaned forward, squinted my eyes.

The darkness shifted. The figure turned and walked out of the room. A jolt ran through me and my muscles went slack.

I willed myself out of bed and into a pair of pants. I ran out into the living room and scanned the house, heart racing. Nothing. I put my hands on my knees and sucked air. Between the nightmares and all the jogging, I was going to have a heart attack.

A cool breeze reached out and caressed my forehead. My skin drank it in. It felt amazing. But then the coolness turned ice cold as I wondered where the breeze came from. I looked up and saw the front door swing closed.

I approached with caution, tentatively touched the knob as if the house was on fire. It felt icy like my sweat. I held my breath and turned, nice and slow. Opened the door two inches and put my fingers into empty space. When I peeked through I saw nothing. So I forced myself to open it the rest of the way and step out onto the front lawn.

There stood the Spaceman, his back to me, in exactly the spot my father had died. He seemed to be looking into the night sky. I followed his gaze to the white dot of Jupiter.

"Dad? Is that you?"

No response. I inched forward.

"Dad?" I called again, my voice thin.

In the light of the moon I finally got a good look at the Spaceman. The suit he wore wasn't one of those bulky modern numbers you see in NASA press shots. It looked more like a biker's road leathers with a breathing apparatus strapped to it. Stylized ribbing ran all along the arms and legs. The helmet resembled a modified motorcycle helmet as opposed to the stereotypical "fish-bowl" design. Oddest of all, the entire suit was tomato red.

I reached out a hand and placed it on the Spaceman's shoulder, where reflective silver stripes accented the suit. I felt nothing of the person inside, only the rhythmic in/out of ventilated breathing. I doubted the wearer of the suit even registered my touch.

I stood like that for a moment, unsure of what to do. I matched the Spaceman breath for breath, our chests rising and falling in unison. My heartbeat slowed. I felt his weight shift as he turned towards me.

"Alan?"

My second startle of the night. I whirled to find Millie walking towards me in her pajamas. Reality accompanied her intrusion. I turned back to the Spaceman, but there was nobody there. My outstretched arm still hung in the air.

"Are you alright?" Millie said. I eased my arm down and turned back around. Confusion and embarrassment fought for dominance inside me.

"Sure," I heard myself say. "Just getting some air."

She wasn't buying it.

"I didn't mean to be nosey. I saw you from the window and wanted to make sure you were all right. After what happened to your father..."

My father? What was she talking about. I drifted off again.

"Are you sure you're okay?"

"You didn't see anyone else out here, did you?"

As spaced out as I was, I could see the concern in her eyes.

"No. You were wandering across the yard, like you were sleepwalking. Then you reached your arm out like this..." She reached out her arm to demonstrate. "Were you following someone?"

I looked back to the spot where my father had died, where the Spaceman had stood only moments earlier.

"No," I said. "I suppose not."

—

I debated telling Max about the episode, but no one else would understand. Except for Millie, who seemed to understand perfectly, but I'd embarrassed myself enough in front of her. It would have to be Max. I decided to spring it on him, casual like. *You'll never guess who I ran into...* I found him sitting on the living room couch making notes with a pen and pad. Perfect opportunity.

"I saw Dad last night," I told him.

"What?" He looked up while his hand continued to scribble. I didn't give him time to digest what I'd said, which meant not giving myself time to chicken out.

"At least I think it was Dad. I didn't get a good look at his face."

Max looked back down to his looping hand. So much for the element of surprise. I wouldn't get a more honest reaction out of him than that.

"I'm starting to worry about you, Albert. Am I gonna have to get you a room next to Mom?"

"I'm being serious."

"So am I. You should have gone for a psych evaluation instead of a physical."

Of course that's the first place he went, sitting there with his fucking pad and pen. Throw in a plywood stand with "Psychiatric Help - 5 Cents" painted across the top and the transformation would be complete.[47] Then he'd pull the football away as I went to kick it and send me flying across the room. Or something like that. I turned to leave. Max called after me.

"Come on, man. You're stressed. You've been thinking about Dad. It was obviously some sort of Freudian nightmare."

He could push buttons with the best of them. Namely: Dad. I whirled on him.

"Freudian? You're the one boasting about how virile you are, telling girls half your age you've been flying around in a metaphorical rocket ship."

Million Dollar Max flashed me his veneers.

---

[47] How come people who've never seen a psychiatrist are always so quick to recommend one? Charles Shultz was right. He had the value of psychiatry pegged from the start.

"Yeah, but from your point of view that rocket ship is your penis, which I stole from you. It's a subconscious manifestation of your feelings of sexual inadequacy."

I grit my teeth. God, I hated him.

"Fuck off," I said, which is exactly what I should have done, fucked off right on out of there, but I couldn't let him win. Not this time.

"Seriously though." He seemed to soften a bit. "If it wasn't a dream, what other logical explanation is there?"

I didn't know, and I sucked at lying. Plus Max was a human lie detector, at least when it came to me.

"There, you see? Dad would be rolling in his grave if he knew you were entertaining the notion of him as a ghost."

Is that what I really thought? The Spaceman was the ghost of my dead father? Who else could it be, a future version of Max? One Max was plenty, thank you very much. Besides, that would make the Spaceman a time traveler, not a ghost. An even harder pill to swallow, one that came with its own set of time-related paradoxes.[48]

"This isn't the first time I've seen him since the funeral," I said.

---

[48] The most Freudian one of all being the grandfather paradox, in which the traveler goes back in time and kills their grandfather to prevent their own birth. This leaves open the potential for all sorts of sordid possibilities, including becoming your own grandmother/grandfather. (In his story "All You Zombies," Robert Heinlein takes this idea a few steps further, when he has the traveler, who has had sexual reassignment surgery, impregnate themselves, thus becoming their own father *and* mother.) Robert Zemeckis played with a variation of this icky theme in *Back to the Future*, which, along with *Star Wars*, seemed to normalize incest in popular culture during the 1980s.

Max clicked his pen against his teeth, then wagged it at me like a head-shrinking pro. "Let me ask you this. Have you spoken to him?"

I shook my head.

"I tried. He didn't say anything back."

Max put the pen back in his mouth.

"Well, that does sound like Dad…"

I told myself to stop there, to drop the whole conversation and go to bed. But I still had another round in the chamber and, oh look, there's a perfectly good foot…

"He was wearing a spacesuit."

Toes exploded everywhere.

"A spacesuit?"

I nodded my head yes. I'd managed to surprise Max twice in one night. A new record.

"Why would a ghost be wearing a spacesuit?"

I shrugged my shoulders.

"Didn't you say Dad worked for NASA?"

The conversation was really going off the rails now.

"As a number cruncher. What do you think, spacesuits were part of the dress code?"

I didn't tell him the spacesuit matched the one in *A Space Odyssey*.[49]

"I guess you're right."

Max looked down at his notepad and shook his head in amusement.

"I can't believe we're having this conversation."

And then his pen flew across the paper like we hadn't.

---

[49] FYI: A replica *2001* red spacesuit does not come cheap.

THE THIRD TWIN
by MILLICENT BLACKFORD

I hadn't been back to creative writing since the critique group debacle. I'd barely been to school at all. Nothing fulfilled me more than writing and literature, but college had turned those things into a chore. I'm sure everyone mocked my thin skin during my absence, but so what? Fuck those guys. And fuck Professor Gables. I didn't need to be beaten down and forced into literary battle, like some sort of word-wielding gladiatrix. I had confidence in my skill. I needed career guidance. I needed an *in*.

I needed to talk to Max.

I felt bad about what happened to poor Mr. Langley, but I couldn't pass up such a tailor made opportunity. Would it make me a hypocrite if I played off Max's obvious interest in me? He had an inherent sleaziness, but he wasn't without his charm. Professor Gables would approve, I'm sure.

I needed to let off some steam, so I considered it serendipity when I ran into Alan on his way out for what looked like a run. I almost didn't recognize him in his sweats and ball cap. In retrospect, I think he actually put his head down and tried to walk past me, hoping I wouldn't. But at the time I didn't even consider he might be avoiding me. I called his name, and he acknowledged my presence with a wan smile, so different from his brother's.

"I didn't know you liked to jog."

"I don't." He made a face. "Doctor's orders."

"You mind if I join you? I could really use a dopamine boost, and they say exercising with a partner improves results. Let me just change real quick."

Before he had a chance to say no I'd changed into my running clothes. Was this how it felt to be the dominant sibling? I could see the appeal. Instead of empathizing with Alan, I took advantage of the situation. We'd run almost a mile before I noticed his hyperventilating. I stopped at a bench so he could catch his breath. I wanted to ask about Max, but I didn't want to jump right into it. I needed to let the conversation happen naturally.

"Going back to work soon?" I asked him.

"We'll see." He pushed the words out between huffs. "I took a leave of absence to sell the house, but since Max moved in…"

He made it too easy.

"You guys getting along?"

Alan shrugged, or maybe it was a dry heave.

"For the most part."

"Everything else is cool?"

"Yeah."

I couldn't help but smile.

"We're just gonna pretend like I didn't find you standing on the front lawn in the middle of the night?"

Alan laughed, leaned back against the bench.

"It's for the best."

I put my hand on his arm. He looked down at it, pleasantly surprised, which made me feel bad, made me want to take it off, but I resisted the urge. For the sake of my career.

"You let me know if you need to talk about it, okay?"

Alan smiled. "Will do."

I got back to my feet.

"Come on, old man. Think you can keep up?" If I'd learned anything about the Langley brothers these past couple weeks, it was that they responded best to one thing — competition.[50]

---

[50] As someone who has since experienced stalking herself, I hope Millie sees the irony in this whole scenario.

BREAKFAST WITH THE MONOLITH by MAX LANGLEY

Paul and Florence Langley stare through nursery glass at their infant sons. Twins, identical to each other in every way, save for the ropey lump of flesh protruding from the diaper of the one. Not attached to its stomach, a desiccated remnant of the umbilical cord, but a congenital mutation of the caudal eminence. A tail.

In fact, if it weren't for the tail, it would be difficult to tell the difference between the pair and the dozen other newborns surrounding them in their bassinets. The doctor had assured the Langleys it was nothing to worry about, and promised he'd throw in what he referred to as "the third circumcision" for free.

Paul takes in the inert mass and frowns. Florence sees the reflection of her husband's face in the glass, superimposed over the child in godlike disapproval. It blackens, losing definition. The more she stares the darker it gets, until it becomes a matte slab blocking out her son. The man-sized monolith swallows the light, a fugue of howling wind and ominous droning emanating from within. A thousand voices crying out in space — "Requiem" by Gyorgy Ligeti. She tries to avert her gaze but can't. She looks deep inside and sees her family's future.

The twins, now toddlers, play in a sandbox.

Paul walks over, plants a plastic rocket on the sand between them. He sits on a bench next to Florence and watches the twins fight over the toy. His wife turns to him, ready to reprimand, but is greeted by the sight of the monolith. The wind picks up, whipping sand and hair, and the horrible droning begins. She bites her tongue and turns her attention back to the children. The monolith's fury subsides.

Later that evening—or is it a week or a month?—Florence busies herself around the kitchen preparing supper. The man-sized monolith stands at the head of the table, its droning dialed down to a mere susurration. The boys avoid looking directly at the imposing slab. A radio on the counter plays the opening fanfare of *Also Sprach Zarathustra* by Richard Strauss.

Twin #2 considers the spoon in his hand. He looks back and forth between the utensil and his brother, an idea forming in his primitive brain. The monolith's droning increases, low end filling the room. As the music on the radio reaches a crescendo, Twin #2 rears back and smacks Twin #1 in the back of the head with the spoon.

da-DUN! Da da duuuuuuuun duuuuuuuun da da duuuuuuuuuuuuuuuuuun!!!

The radio blares major key triumphant. Twin #1 bursts into tears. Florence glares at his brother.

"What did you do this time?"

She scoops up Twin #1 and whisks him towards the other room. She calls out to the monolith as she goes.

"You're supposed to be watching them, not observing them. There's a difference, you know."

She proceeds to bounce Twin #1 up and down in her arms.

"Sh... it's okay, baby..."

Twin #2 watches his mother go before turning to his father for approval, but receives none. Just the howling expanse of nothingness within the monolith. The child bangs the spoon on the table a few times to amuse himself before launching it into the air. The Florence in the hospital nursery watches the spoon flip end over end in slow motion.

Even later that evening—or is it years that have passed now?— the man-sized monolith lies on a recliner in front of the TV. The fugue of "Requiem" emanates from within. Or is the television the source of the sound?

We see the monolith for what it really is, Paul Langley, passed out drunk on the recliner, watching *2001: A Space Odyssey*. "Requiem" blares from the device's single speaker. The twins, now pre-teens, sneak up behind the recliner to watch the movie, careful not to wake their father. The monolith on the screen stares out at them from the foot of Bowman's bed. Within its darkness floats Florence's face, still watching from the nursery.

Florence doesn't understand what she sees but keeps watching. The setting changes to an old motel room. The "William Tell Overture" by Rossini plays on a phonograph. Her husband, Paul, has sex with a variety of women in an undercranked movie montage. He gets older while they remain young. A red spacesuit lies draped over a chair in the corner, like hastily discarded clothes. One of the women, a girl next door type, looks eerily like a younger version of his neighbor, Mrs. Blackford.

Another abrupt scene change. The man-sized black monolith stands in the front yard of the Langley home. The fugue of "Requiem" emanates from within. Jupiter is visible in the night sky. Florence sees the pinpoint of light reflected in the monolith, reflected in the nursery glass.

Cut to the interior of a room in a nursing home. Florence recognizes an elderly version of herself asleep in bed under the watchful eye of a large crucifix. Paul Langley, now in his 70s, sits across from her, wearing a black suit, sans shoes and socks.

Cut to Paul's room back home where her adult son, Albert, sleeps on a stained mattress. A Figure in a red spacesuit watches over him from the foot of the bed. Albert's muscles tense and sweat beads down his face.

Cut to Oak Grove Cemetery that very same day. The man-sized monolith lies flat on its back in place of a coffin. It has lost some of its shine and cracks have appeared in its facade. The crucifix from Florence's room adorns its chest. The fugue is silent.

The minister delivers the eulogy. Eight year old Albert sits next to elderly Mrs. Langley in the front row, cradling a withered rope of flesh in his lap. Mrs. Blackford and her adult daughter, Millie, sit next to them. Chimps in black suits make up the remaining mourners. They show uncharacteristic reverence.

In the distance, a rocket ship stands among the tombstones. Its design recalls a miniature from an old sci-fi flick, or a children's toy. A man in a red spacesuit walks down a set of stairs and approaches the burial. He takes off the helmet to reveal himself as Max Langley, Paul's other son, the adult version of Albert's twin.

Millie sees Max and runs towards him, black dress flowing behind her. She leaps into his arms and they share a warm embrace while young Albert looks on. He grips the rope of flesh tight in his tiny hand. This is intercut with brief flashes of young Albert, bent over his mother's knee, flinching as she brings the ropey length of his umbilical cord down across his bare buttocks again and again.

The vision ends, leaving Florence staring at her own reflection in the glass of the nursery. The monolith has morphed back into Paul, who turns and walks away without a word. Both children spontaneously burst into tears.

THE PARADOX TWINS
by ALBERT LANGLEY

My life regained a semblance of normalcy. Although now that I think about it, that's a little misleading. My life had never been normal, so there was nothing to regain. Which, to me, made my current normalcy seem like even more of an accomplishment.

Things with Max were going well. Granted, he spent most of his time holed up in Dad's office doing research, but we managed to cohabitate without resorting to blows. I actually looked forward to his company each evening. We'd sit and watch *2001* at least a couple times a week. Max studied it, like it held a key to the mystery of our father. I found myself appreciating the film in a whole new light, picking up on previously innocuous details, ascribing them meaning based on my own experiences.[51]

And physically I felt great. I'd started eating better, and the running—I considered running my fountain of youth. When you're an out of shape slob, you can't stand hearing

---

[51] I wonder if they ever attempted to sync the Stargate Sequence with Pink Floyd's "Echoes." As (urban) legend has it, the band purposefully wrote the song to said sequence to get back at Kubrick for turning down their supposed offer to score *2001*. Despite this being a combination of misinformation, bunk, and total hearsay, the two do sync together quite nicely.

One of my earliest memories is of lying in my crib with "Echoes" on in the background. According to my mother I was a very colicky baby, and nothing quieted me down/drowned me out better than Pink Floyd.

people preach about their fitness regime, but once you've established your own it becomes an addiction. I actually looked forward to my daily run. I *needed* it. And having Millie as a partner helped big time. It didn't even feel like work. It felt like something I did for fun. And I think she enjoyed it too. I wasn't a pet project for her. And she was so easy to talk to. She became my miracle worker, my own little Annie Sullivan. Does that sound trite? I'm not trying to equate being a few pounds overweight to living without sight or sound. I just can't understate Millie's involvement.

Now I know what you're thinking. This doesn't sound like me at all. Well, you're right. And the only reason I've delved so deep into the good times is to highlight how bad they were about to become.

I had finished a run with Millie and I was riding high on endorphins. I'd shifted gears into cooldown mode and coasted into the house for some well deserved kombucha (fucking KOMBUCHA, I know). Feeling extra brotherly, I poked my head into the study to see if Max wanted one.[52] He wasn't there, which I found odd, but he'd left his laptop open. Maybe he'd stepped out for coffee or something. I was all set to go hit the shower when before you know it I found myself sitting in front of the computer. A file on the desktop entitled *Breakfast with the Monolith* drew my attention. I knew I shouldn't, but I couldn't help myself. I clicked the icon.

---

[52] This seems like a big no-no to me, as Max is/was in recovery and kombucha, being fermented, contains a small amount of alcohol. Once an alcoholic, always an alcoholic, and all it takes is a taste. I never touch the stuff. Fucks with my meds.

Big mistake.

Disappointment overwhelmed me. And I'm not talking about the prose here (although, to be fair, I found it a tad over-written). No wonder Max was being so nice—he was mining our family history for memoir fodder right under my nose. The further I read, the tighter my stomach twisted. How could I have been so naive?

I don't know how much time had gone by between when I finished reading and Max came home, but that's how he found me—staring at the screen in shock.

"Hey, brother..." It sounded innocent enough, but he had his war face on. I jabbed a finger at the computer screen, hard enough to cause a rainbow colored ripple in the LCD.

"What the fuck is this?"

He held up both hands, palms upwards, the posture of a hostage negotiator.

"Easy there. It looks like an invasion of privacy, but you tell me."

"You used me." I slammed the laptop shut to drive my point home. Max winced.

"What are you talking about?" He inched closer, trying to put himself within grabbing distance of the computer. I got to my feet.

"This isn't a memoir, it's a complete fabrication! All this metaphysical nonsense about Dad being a stoic, emotionless slab—it's pure science fiction!"

"Alright, I admit the project has undergone some changes…"

"And all that shit about the Spaceman... I told you that stuff in confidence."

"You thought I wasn't going to use that? It's literary gold!"

"It makes me look like an idiot!"

"Calm down. No one's going to take it as fact."

"You gave me a fucking tail!"

"What's the big deal? Everyone knows you weren't born with a tail."

Everyone *didn't* know I wasn't born with a tail. And once you put an idea like that in someone's head, you can't take it back. It's like falsely accusing someone of a terrible crime.[53] Even if they're exonerated, there will always be that *What if?* in the back of people's minds. But people thinking I had a tail wasn't my main concern.

"All this stuff about Millie... it has nothing to do with the story."

Max cocked his head at me. "It doesn't?"

He had me there and he knew it. I decided to change tactics, appeal to his... humanity? Sense of decency? As far as I knew, Max possessed neither.

"I can't believe how selfish you are."

Max's face softened, but that didn't fool me. I knew what came next. The part in the argument where he placated me, played devil's advocate against his own ideas in an attempt to make me feel guilty. I was the bad guy for not letting him run my name through the shit. I was the selfish one.

---

[53] The reason so many people are afraid of polite interaction with their fellow man. Try to get to know the wrong person and BAM! You could be branded a creep for the rest of your life.

"Look, my publisher wants a novel," he said. "They think I can cross over to the adult market with this. So what it's not a memoir? It's still about Dad and there's still truth in it."

It was a manipulative tactic, one that usually worked. He'd learned from the best. Good old predictable me, I felt myself giving in as I opened my mouth.

"I want you out of here." The words surprised both of us. It took Max a few seconds to recover.

"Come on, Al, don't be like that."

I doubled down before I lost my nerve.

"Pack your shit. Now."

The alpha male turned into a meek forest creature as the reality of the situation sank in.

"Fine. I've gotten everything I need here."

Max reached for his laptop but I wouldn't let go. I wanted to look him in the eye, so he could see how serious I was. We stood that way for a moment before he tugged again and I released my grip. He put the computer under his arm and walked away, pausing in the doorway.

"I'll be at the hotel if you change your mind."

And then he left.

I fell back into the chair and hung my head in my hands. I didn't pick it up again until I heard the front door slam. When I did the colors in the room seemed a little less bright.

I looked around Dad's office for some insight, some sort of magic epiphany to jump out from behind a bookshelf and tell me what to do next. Max had packed up most of Dad's notes. For all I knew he had plagiarized Dad's unpublished "novel."

And then my eyes came to rest on the box of Polaroids.

I picked up a handful and went through them. There had to be something here, I thought, but all I saw were pictures of dad with different women. Blondes, brunettes, black, white—one of the few areas in which it seems he didn't discriminate. Most of the shots were casual, post coital. They possessed a documentary-like quality, like I was looking at a stranger, not my own father. I was an anonymous voyeur, impersonal. I got about halfway through the stack before I saw it.

A picture of dad and Mrs. Blackford.

She looked a lot younger, but I recognized her immediately. I could see a lot of Millie in her.

I can see a lot of me in Millie! the Dad in my mind said. But for once, he wasn't being euphemistic.[54]

Oh shit. Millie.

---

[54] You know the old joke about married couples starting to look like each other? Maybe there's something to that. Millie touched on this during the lasagna sit-down. Say constant proximity resulted in some sort of aesthetic homogenization. That could also explain the reverse—why separated twins might not look alike. Or why a child who never knew their father bore no resemblance to the man, which, now that I think about it, makes the situation that much sadder.

THE THIRD TWIN
by MILLICENT BLACKFORD

One run with Alan and I became his exercise partner. I couldn't walk to the mailbox without him pulling up alongside me in sweats and a hoodie, raring to go. I guess it served me right. I had initiated the whole thing in a selfish attempt to get closer to his brother and further my career. Besides, his spirits were up and physically he looked a whole lot better. I considered it karma in the bank.

We sat at our usual bench, catching our breath, when he told he'd kicked Max out. My first thought was, *I hope Max hasn't left town*, but out loud I said something to the effect of, "Oh my god, what happened?" I touched Alan's arm, which usually kept the conversation ball rolling, but this time he pulled away. Seemed he had built up an immunity to my feminine wiles.

"The book," he said. "There were... creative differences."

A strange statement, because as far as I knew, the project wasn't a collaboration. I intended to say as much, but arm-touch or no arm-touch, he kept talking.

"I objected to his portrayal of my father." *My*. Not *our*. He paused dramatically to look me in the eye. "Me as well."

"I mean, it's his book, right?" I trailed off, hoping he'd keep going, but he lapsed into silence. The next time he spoke, he had changed the subject entirely.

"Were you close with your father?"

It took me a moment to adjust to this sudden pivot.

"I never knew my father. He and my mother separated a year after I was born."

"Do you remember *anything* about him?"

I flashed back to the distorted face from my dream, twisted with sunspots, this time accompanied by a quavering howl.

"Not really. Mom refuses to talk about it. Every time I bring it up, she changes the subject."

Alan nodded his head like he knew and that's when it hit me. Maybe he did know. He grew up next door, he had to have known my father. I took a controlled breath before asking.

"Did you ever meet him?"

I saw the answer in his eyes before he said a word. I also saw how sad it made him to tell me.

"No. I mean, it's... possible. But not that I remember. I was away at college, and that was around the time of my parent's divorce, so I didn't come home very often."

"Oh." Highlighting our age difference made things even more awkward. But that paled in comparison to the awkwardness to come.

"But I know someone who probably did."

—

I did the math in my head on the way to the nursing home. Alan said his parents got divorced in 1986, about a year after I was born. As far as I could recall his father had always lived alone. Still, the possibility existed...

Alan knocked lightly as he opened the door to his mother's room.

"Mom? I brought you a visitor."

A frail woman sat upright in bed, staring out the window. It had already started to get dark, and aside from a few trees, the view didn't offer much. She had no television and only one book—a leather-bound bible that sat on the nightstand. She turned and looked me up and down as we entered the room.

"She's a bit young for you, don't you think?" The venom in her voice belied her meek appearance. Alan put a hand against my back as if he thought the words might knock me down. He ushered me over to a chair by the bed.

"No, this is Millie from next door. Mrs. Blackford's daughter, remember?"

"Oh." Florence turned back to the window. "Tell her to take her shoes off."

She didn't seem to recognize me. Not a good sign. I looked to Alan for direction.

"Should I?" I mouthed. He shook his head no and sat down next to me.

"We're not gonna stay long."

We sat there in silence. I didn't know where to put my eyes. A bird alighted on a tree branch outside, but Mrs. Langley didn't appear to notice.

"So," Alan said. "Have you spoken to Dad recently?"

I looked away involuntarily, even though Mrs. Langley wasn't facing us. I knew Alan hadn't told his mother about the funeral, but the question seemed cruel. A cruelty matched only by the answer.

"Your father's dead to me."

I gave Alan a stern look, but he only smiled. It might as well have been a wink. *Don't worry, I fuck with her all the time.* I felt complicit in some sort of mean-spirited trick.

"He's dead to a lot of people these days. But have you, you know, *seen* him?"

"I've seen him. Told him not to come around any more. I want nothing to do with him."

This was too much. I got up to leave, but Alan held out his hand.

"I'll explain later," he said to me. Then, to Mrs. Langley: "What do you think he wants?"

"He don't want nothin'. He just sits there without speaking. Some things never change."

"And he's always wearing his suit? You've never seen him dressed like... oh, I don't know, an astronaut or anything like that?"

Mrs. Langley turned to glare at her son, eyes narrowed into slits.

"What kind of nonsense is that? Is that why you're here? To harass me like your father did?"

Alan backed down.

"You're right, I'm sorry. I... we're actually here to talk about Millie's father."

Mrs. Langley turned back to the window.

"I don't know nothin' about it."

Well, that was a bust. I wanted to throw in the towel, but Alan pressed the issue.

"Are you sure, Mom? You had to have met the man."

"I said I don't know nothing about it!" Her voice filled the room. Loud and strong for such a frail woman.

"We should go," I said. "You're upsetting her."

Alan continued to press the issue.

"Mrs. Blackford never said anything to you? You guys never discussed it over tea?"

Florence Langley gripped the duvet with boney fingers, balled them into a pair of fists.

"That bitch never said nothin'!" She gave the duvet a good shake. "Now take that little tramp of hers and get the hell out of here!"

I stormed out of the room. Looking back, Alan knew what he was doing. The same thing his family always did — push each other's buttons. And, as usually seemed the case, the sweetest victory involved witnesses. An audience to perform for. He may have taken me to visit his mother out of a genuine desire to help, but he lost sight of that along the way and the visit turned into an interrogation. I think his mother's outburst shocked him as much as it shocked me, because as I fled the room I heard his surprised intake of breath.

———

Halfway across the parking lot Alan finally caught up with me.

"Hey, Millie, wait up."

But I had no intention of stopping. I didn't even know if I was headed in the right direction. My plan was to walk in a straight line until my anger subsided.

"I told you not to push her," I said without slowing down.

"I know. I'm sorry. I've never seen her like that. She's never said a bad word in her life."

"Well she's obviously expanded her vocabulary."

Alan sprinted to close the rest of the gap.

"Come on, I'll take you home." He reached for my arm, but I pulled away.

"I'm gonna walk. I need to clear my head."

Alan stopped. I could tell because I heard only one set of footsteps, my own, echoing angrily off the pavement.

"You sure?" he called after me. "It's a long way back."

"Yeah, I'm sure." I said it under my breath, but he got the message.

I hit the sidewalk and increased my stride. I'm not sure how long he stood there and I didn't care. I marched across Mission Street. The anger combined with my pumping blood propelled my feet. God, I needed a drink. My internal GPS took over and before I knew it I stood outside a pub—*the* pub—awash in neon light. Before I had time to admit to myself what I was doing I walked through the door and stood in front of Max at his corner booth.

"Can we talk?"

He looked up from his writing. The Langley brothers wanted to play games? I could play games. In my ignorance I didn't think I was in over my head.

"Of course," Max said, all teeth like a shark. "Let me get you a drink." [55]

---

[55] Both Florence Langley and Mrs. Blackford are portrayed as such hard women by their children. I wonder how that made them feel? Reminds me of my own mother, may she rest in peace. She died the way she lived: as a complicated woman, full of contradictions. During her final moments she went through a whole range of emotions: fear, resentment, acceptance, and ultimately—at least I'd like to believe— forgiveness.

THE PARADOX TWINS
by ALBERT LANGLEY

Moms are tough. An individual can become so accustomed to their matriarch's particular brand of crazy[56] that they forget what the experience might be like to an outsider. Even if you think the uninitiated can handle it, that doesn't mean the mother in question won't go off script and surprise you with some new and improved lunacy when backed into a corner.

I felt bad about how Mom had treated Millie, so I decided to pay penance by throwing myself at the mercy of her own mother. If anyone knew the truth about Millie's lineage, Mrs. Blackford did. Whether she would divulge the info or not was another matter.

I knocked on the Blackford's front door and took a step back. In my eagerness to be the one to provide Millie with the information she so desperately wanted, I had gone in without a game plan. As soon as the old woman opened the door and I saw her steely gaze, I realized I'd made a huge mistake.

Where to begin? How about getting inside the house, dummy? Mrs. Blackford regarded me coolly, waiting for me to make the first move, and I was blowing it. I finally managed to get the words out.

---

[56] Certain research suggests mental illness is hereditary. Chances of developing bipolar disorder or schizophrenia increase over 50% if both parents suffered from the same illness. The highest at risk group? Siblings of identical twins with mental illness, at up to 80 or 90%.

"Hello, Mrs. Blackford."

"Hello, Alan. I'm afraid Millie's not home."

She wasn't making things easy.

"That's okay. I'm actually here to see you. May I come in?"

She raised a single eyebrow but didn't move. She stood, legs braced, her shoulders centered in the doorway. Her posture made it clear I wasn't welcome.

Yet somehow I found myself sitting across from her in the kitchen, a pair of hot teas between us. I looked around the room, stalling. I don't think I'd ever been inside the house before. Mrs. Blackford indulged me only a moment, before reminding me I wasn't there on a social call.

"What did you want to speak to me about, Mr. Langley? If it's about the lasagna, I don't give out the recipe."[57]

Was that a joke? I couldn't tell. Her face remained an inscrutable mask.

"No, of course not. It's about Millie."

Mrs. Blackford pursed her lips.

"If you don't mind my saying so, Mr. Langley, I find your friendship with my daughter troubling. What could a man of your age possibly have in common with a girl so young?"

Mrs. Blackford didn't mince words. She was going for the kill right out the gate. But somehow I found the right words and heard myself say them.

"Well, actually, Mrs. Blackford, that's what I'm here to find out."

---

[57] Not true. Mrs. Blackford allowed Millie to print the recipe in *The Third Twin*. You may have even seen Millie on the cooking segment of a morning show or two.

"Oh?" I think my confidence surprised her. I plunged in head-first while I had the advantage.

"The death of my father has got me thinking about family a lot and I wanted to ask... I never knew Millie's father—"

"We divorced when Millie was young."

"Millie said she was still a baby."

"Yes. You had just graduated college, I believe?"

My admiration took the form of a smile.

"You have a good memory."

She responded with detached observation. I continued.

"She says every time she brings him up you change the subject."

"Are you going anywhere with this?"

"Yes, I... It's just... do you have a picture of Mr. Blackford I could see?"

Mrs. Blackford looked down at me, a high-angle gaze from a position of power. Was her chair taller than mine? Did she do that on purpose? Vulnerability permeated my defenses. She'd gone all Sun Tzu on me.

"Mr. Langley. This is a personal matter between me and my daughter. You may not understand them, but I have perfectly good reasons why I don't want Millie to know about her father, and frankly, they are none of your business." The old woman got to her feet, signaling an end to our conversation. "Now if you'll excuse me, I have housework to do. Will there be anything else?"

I bowed my head in deference, accepted my defeat.

"No, Mrs. Blackford. I appreciate your time."

She escorted me to the front door. As I walked down the steps she channeled her inner Columbo and hit me with a parting shot.

"One more thing, Mr. Langley."

I turned to take what I had coming.

"I appreciate you taking an interest in my daughter's well being. I don't mind if you feel the need to play the big brother, so to speak. Just make sure you don't step out of line."

She locked me in her high-beam stare. I had no response.

INT. LAWYER'S OFFICE - DAY

Alan sits across the desk from a flab-
bergasted Todd.

> TODD
> You want to do what?!?!

> ALAN
> Dig him up. Unless there's
> another way.

Todd shakes his head.

> TODD
> You realize how hard it is to get
> a court order to exhume a body?

> ALAN
> You don't think the situation
> warrants it?

> TODD
> Is the party contesting the will?

                    ALAN
No. I don't think she has any
idea.

                    TODD
Then no, I don't think the
situation warrants digging up
your father's corpse to do a
DNA test.

                    ALAN
                (disappointed)
Can you use toenail clippings? I
might still have some back at the
house. Or an old toothbrush.
Or, wait a minute--what about…
                (lowers voice)
...fecal stains?

Todd laughs out loud.

                    TODD
As amusing as this is, there
is an easier way.

                    ALAN
What?

                    TODD
Though not as conclusive, a test
against any close living relative
will do.

                    ALAN
You mean like me?

                    TODD
Yes. Like you. All you'll need is
a sample from the individual in
question.

EXT. BLACKFORD HOUSE - DAY

Mrs. Blackford opens the door to find
Alan on her stoop.

                    MRS. BLACKFORD
What do you want, Mr. Langley?

                    ALAN
We're having some plumbing
problems over at Casa de Langley.
Think I could use your bathroom?

INT. BLACKFORD BATHROOM - DAY

Alan shuts the door behind him and scans
the room. It is impeccably clean. Unfortunately he doesn't see a toothbrush.
He checks inside the medicine cabinet.
Nothing. He goes for the garbage. Empty.

                    ALAN
        Shit.

He opens the bathroom door and peers
into the hallway. He can hear the
sounds of Mrs. Blackford puttering in
the kitchen. He closes the door behind him and makes a break for it.

INT. BLACKFORD HOUSE - CONTINUOUS

Alan makes his way upstairs, quiet as
possible. He locates the second floor
bathroom.

INT. MILLIE'S BATHROOM - CONTINUOUS

Alan contemplates Millie's toothbrush. He puts it down and checks
the waste basket. A balled-up wad of
toilet paper seeps dark red.

Alan surveys the bathroom for something to wrap it in. A solitary shred
of toilet paper hangs from the card-
board roll. His only other option — a
nice, clean white hand towel.

He grimaces and reaches for the refuse. He extracts the bundle with two
dainty fingers.

INT. BLACKFORD HOUSE - KITCHEN

Mrs. Blackford continues to putter
around the kitchen.

INT. MILLIE'S BATHROOM - DAY

Alan exits the bathroom and makes for
the stairs, holding the wad at arm's
length. He pauses as he passes the
doorway to--

INT. MILLIE'S BEDROOM - CONTINUOUS

He forgets the refuse in hand as
he surveys the room. His eyes come
across a copy of "WAR FOR ANTHROPICA"
on Millie's dresser. He opens the
book to find an inscription. It reads:

"TO MY NEW FAVORITE FAN --MAX"

Below the inscription is Max's cell number.[58] Alan frowns.

The sound of FOOTSTEPS from downstairs brings him back to reality.

INT. BLACKFORD HOUSE - CONTINUOUS

Alan peers down the stairs. Mrs. Blackford stands outside the first floor bathroom. She puts her ear to the door. Alan can't believe what he sees.

After she walks away, Alan hurries down the stairs on tip-toes. As he reaches the first floor landing, he drops the tuft of toilet paper behind him.

                    ALAN
               (whispers)
          Shit.

---

[58] The inscription actually read, "To my *future* favorite fan," (an odd distinction), and did not include a phone number. Years later Millie auctioned the book off for charity, and donated all proceeds to RAINN.

Alan pauses, pivots, and reaches down to snatch up the stolen refuse. He returns to the safety of the first floor bathroom. He is closing the door when he notices the drop of blood on the landing.

                    ALAN
                (whispers)
          Shit shit shit.

Alan tip-toes quick and quiet, re-tracing his steps to the errant spot. He reaches down and wipes it with the tissue, leaving a big dark smear.

He looks at the toilet tissue, then back to the smear, paralyzed by in-decision. FOOTSTEPS are once again heading in his direction.

He bends down, licks his thumb, and rubs it against the floor, scrunching his nose. He then wipes the spot with his palm for good measure, bolts for the bathroom and shuts the door.

INT. BLACKFORD BATHROOM - DAY

Alan pulls a generous helping of toilet paper off the roll and wraps his specimen.

INT. BLACKFORD HOUSE - DAY

Mrs. Blackford listens to the vigorous sounds of Alan washing his hands.

INT. BLACKFORD BATHROOM - DAY

Alan shoves the bundle into his pocket and takes a calming breath.

INT. BLACKFORD HOUSE - CONTINUOUS

A nonchalant Alan exits the bathroom, under the watchful eye of Mrs. Blackford.

                    ALAN
        You have a good day, Mrs.
        Blackford.

She eyeballs him as he speed walks to the door.

INT. DOCTOR'S OFFICE - DAY

Alan and the Doctor sit across from one another. The wadded up toilet tissue sits on the desk between them.

> DOCTOR
> This is... highly unorthodox.

> ALAN
> But it *would* be possible to conduct a DNA test using this sample?

> DOCTOR
> Well, yes, it's possible, but there are legal issues.

> ALAN
> Such as?

> DOCTOR
> Such as... how did you say you acquired this sample again?

> ALAN
> I got it from my neighbor's bathroom.

                    DOCTOR
          Right. That right there.
          That's what I'm talking about.

                     ALAN
          What? It was in the garbage.
          Isn't trash public property?

                    DOCTOR
          On the street it is.

                     ALAN
          Semantics.

The doctor throws up his hands.

                    DOCTOR
          I'm sorry. I'm not comfortable
          with this. I can't legally
          perform the test without written
          consent from both parties.

                     ALAN
          What if I got the tampon
          notarized?

The doctor sighs.

                    DOCTOR
        I shouldn't be encouraging you,
        but you are aware you can buy
        DNA tests over the counter now?

                    ALAN
        You can?

                    DOCTOR
        Yes. And most home tests only
        require a simple buccal swab. Now
        please get the hell out
        of my office.

INT. PHARMACY - DAY

Alan tries to look inconspicuous as
he browses the family planning aisle.
He picks up a paternity test. The
box features a smiling woman holding
an infant. The ad copy boasts: "NOW
COURT ADMISSIBLE!"

An inert PHARMACY EMPLOYEE wanders
into the aisle.

                    PHARMACY EMPLOYEE
        Oh, hey Mr. L! What are you doing?
        Shopping for jimmies?

ALAN

What? No, I-- Wait a minute, do I
know you? Are you a student of mine?

PHARMACY EMPLOYEE

Nelson Randolph.[59] Graduated a few
years ago?

Alan goes back to browsing.

ALAN

Right. Nelson. I remember you.

PHARMACY EMPLOYEE

Oh man, I can't wait to tell
everyone I helped Mr. L pick
out some condoms.

ALAN

That's not what's going on here.

PHARMACY EMPLOYEE
(grinning)

I get it. Keepin' it on the DL.
What did you have in mind? Ultra
thin? Extra Large? Ribbed for her--

[59] No listing for Nelson Randolph exists in any Boston school records, further confirming my suspicion this section is a complete fabrication. A Randy Jimson of Central Falls, RI once claimed the character to be based on him, but never provided any proof.

                    ALAN
                (getting frustrated)
          Look, can you shut up for a
          minute? I have a question about
          these paternity tests. Do you
          know if they also test for
          siblingship?

The employee gives him a weird look.

                    ALAN (CONT'D)
          You know, siblings? Brother and
          sister?

                    PHARMACY EMPLOYEE
          Uh, it's really none of my busi-
          ness, but I don't think that's
          even legal, man.

                    ALAN
          What?

                    PHARMACY EMPLOYEE
          The whole brother/sister thing.

                    ALAN
          No, that's not what I mean. I'm
          talking about a DNA test that proves
          people are brother and sister.

                    PHARMACY EMPLOYEE
        Oh. Phew. For a second there I
        thought I might have to call my
        manager. I don't know the
        protocol on alerting the
        authorities about that sort of thing.

Alan pauses to consider the employee
more closely.

                    ALAN
        Are you sure YOUR parents weren't
        brother and sister?

The employee makes a face like he's
just been informed he's adopted.

                    PHARMACY EMPLOYEE
        Huh?

                    ALAN
        Never mind.

Alan picks up another paternity test.

                    ALAN (CONT'D)
        You wouldn't happen to know
        whether this test would suit my
        needs, would you?

The employee gives a blank look.

>   ALAN (CONT'D)
>   You know, the brother/sister
>   thing?

>   PHARMACY EMPLOYEE
>   Oh, right. I dunno. You're the
>   scientist, man.

>   ALAN
>   I'm a physics teacher. And now I
>   remember why I failed you.

Alan storms off towards the cash register with the test. The employee waves, unfazed.

>   PHARMACY EMPLOYEE
>   See you around, Mr. L! Don't
>   forget: wrap it before you tap it!

EXT. BLACKFORD HOUSE - DAY

Alan stands at the front door, pharmacy bag in hand. Mrs. Blackford answers.

>   MRS. BLACKFORD
>   Yes, Mr. Langley?

                        ALAN
     Sorry to bother you again, Mrs. Black-
     ford, but can I use the facilities?

Mrs. Blackford narrows her eyes.

                   MRS. BLACKFORD
          Number one or number two?

INT. MILLIE'S BATHROOM - DAY

Alan sneaks into the bathroom and
shuts the door. He opens the bag and
pulls out the paternity test. He skims
the back of the box before tearing it
open. He grabs Millie's toothbrush and
brandishes a mouth swab.

                        ALAN
          Here goes everything.

Alan rubs the swab against the toothbrush bristles.

INT. BLACKFORD HOUSE - CONTINUOUS

Mrs. Blackford confronts Alan as he
sneaks down the stairs, clutching the
pharmacy bag.

MRS. BLACKFORD

Just what the hell do you think
you're doing?

ALAN

Sorry, Mrs. Blackford, I…

MRS. BLACKFORD

You what, Mr. Langley?

ALAN

Well, this is kind of
embarrassing…

MRS. BLACKFORD

Not as embarrassing as it will be
when I call the police.

ALAN

Right. Look, I'm sorry, no need
to get the law involved. It's
just... I didn't want you to hear me.

MRS. BLACKFORD

Hear you?

ALAN

Right. Lunch isn't sitting well and I was
afraid there'd be... bathroom noises.

                    MRS. BLACKFORD
          What do you think I was going to
          do, stand there and listen with
          my ear to the door?

                         ALAN
          Well…

She spies the pharmacy bag.

                    MRS. BLACKFORD
          What's in the bag, Mr. Langley.

                         ALAN
          Excuse me?

                    MRS. BLACKFORD
          The bag. What's in it?

                         ALAN
          Oh, you know, just... pharmacy stuff.

                    MRS. BLACKFORD
          Let me see.

                         ALAN
          It's just a few personal items.
          For my stomach. Again, I'm really
          embarrassed by this whole thing.

Mrs. Blackford advances.

> MRS. BLACKFORD
> I'm a mother, dear. I've seen and heard it all.

> ALAN
> Still, I just... I should really be going.

> MRS. BLACKFORD
> Show me what's in the bag, Albert!

> ALAN
> Really, I just... thank you for your hospitality, but I've got to go.

Alan makes a run for it, but the old lady moves quick. She grabs the bottom of the paper bag and pulls. The bag tears and the box falls to the floor, smiling mom and baby conveniently facing up.

> MRS. BLACKFORD
> I thought I told you this didn't concern you.

                    ALAN
          I'm sorry, Mrs. Blackford, but I
          have to know.

                    MRS. BLACKFORD
          You obviously haven't said any-
          thing to Millie, otherwise you
          wouldn't be skulking around her
          bathroom looking for DNA samples.

                    ALAN
          I wanted to be sure.

Mrs. Blackford studies his face.

                    MRS. BLACKFORD
          You need to ask yourself why
          you're doing this, Mr. Langley.
          Make sure you're being honest
          about your motivations.

                    ALAN
          I... I know.

                    MRS. BLACKFORD
          I have my reasons for not telling
          Millie who her father is.

                    ALAN
        I understand.

                    MRS. BLACKFORD
        Do you? Because from where I'm
        standing, it doesn't seem like it.

                    ALAN
        Don't you think it would be
        better for all of us if you told
        her the truth?

                    MRS. BLACKFORD
        All of us? No, I don't think it
        would. And if you care about
        Millie as much as you claim,
        you'd leave it alone.

        Mrs. Blackford bends down to pick up
        the test. She hands it to Alan.

                    MRS. BLACKFORD
        I think you should go now.

THE PARADOX TWINS
by ALBERT LANGLEY

Getting a sample of Millie's DNA proved easier than expected. I asked Mrs. Blackford to use her bathroom (as we were experiencing "plumbing problems") and rubbed Millie's toothbrush on the buccal swab.[60] I have to admit, it felt intensely intimate, and I seriously questioned going through with the whole plan. I kept coming back to what Mrs. Blackford had said. *This is a personal matter between me and my daughter.* As much as I disagreed with her motives, she was right. But if I proved to be family...didn't I deserve to have a say?

Indecision had a hold of me. I kept thinking of the lyrics to "Freewill" by Rush: *If you choose not to decide you still have made a choice.* The band had written the song about religious belief, but it still applied here. Lee's authoritative falsetto was hard to deny.

I spent whole nights sitting at the kitchen table, staring at an envelope marked "Millie," the one that contained the ill-gotten sample. The kit had also come with a consent form for DNA obtained from the second party. How bad could the legal repercussions be if I forged Millie's signature? The manufacturer probably included the form to cover their ass.

---

[60] Funny how there is nary a mention of digging up corpses or used tampons or confronting ex-students in the family planning aisle in any of the existing memoir accounts. What was the screenwriter thinking when they came up with the borderline farcical subplot about acquiring the DNA sample? It is so tonally off—no wonder this movie never got made.

The deciding factor came via Millie herself. If she had kept her distance, kept out of harm's way, Max would have grown tired of living the suburban lifestyle and moved on. But no, she couldn't leave well enough alone. So when she came to me and told me Max had agreed to mentor her, I knew what I had to do. I knew what "mentor" meant in Max Langley's world.

And even though I'd kicked Max out, I still spent most nights at the house. He was still in town, after all, and I wanted to make sure he left Millie alone. I hadn't seen her since the incident with my mother, and I was still dealing with a lot of residual guilt about that. If Mom hadn't been such a bitch, the whole situation would have been a lot less awkward.

"Haven't seen you in a couple days," Millie said over the fence that divided our properties, if not our lives. She took in my button down shirt and solid color tie. "You back at work?"

How To Initiate Conversation At 100 Paces, by Millie Blackford.[61] I looked up like I'd just realized she was there.

"The little monsters need educating," I said as I approached the fence. I noticed she cradled what looked like a manuscript. "You're not still upset about the other day, are you?"

"Nah. I needed to clear my head is all."

I nodded, shifted my weight from foot to foot. My substantially less weight, weight she'd helped me lose.

---

[61] One industrious internetter managed to get this title listed on Amazon as Millie's follow-up book, a hoax which blew up social media for about half a day.

"Look, I'm sorry about all that. I should've minded my own business."

"You were only trying to help."

Did she mean that? I couldn't get a read on her. Her right leg bounced up and down.

"Well, next time feel free to tell me to butt out."

That got a smile out of her. I had forgotten how good those made me feel.

"I will."

I nodded towards the manuscript.

"What're you reading?"

She handed me the stack of papers. A printout of *Breakfast with the Monolith*. Cue the fucking timpani.

"It's really not that bad," she said.

I tried my best to mask my—hurt? Jealousy? I did a mediocre job.

"You've been to see him?"

"I wanted to make sure he was okay."

"You wanted to make sure HE was okay?" My voice pitched close to a whine.

"Well, full disclosure, I did have an ulterior motive."

Here we go. The situation was worse than I thought. They'd already consummated, heredity be damned! I waited stone-faced for her to continue, my insides a maelstrom of negative energy.

"He's agreed to mentor me."

"Oh." Such a small, vulnerable word. It said more than the whole of our conversation up to that point.

She crinkled her face into an exaggerated mask of anticipation.

"Are you upset?"

"No," I lied. "That's great. Congratulations."

"You're upset."

"I'm not upset. It's just... be careful with my brother, okay? You're not the only one with ulterior motives." I willed as much sincerity into the words as I dared. If I learned nothing else from teaching high school, sincerity was like poison to young people. Go overboard on the concern and they'd run straight into the arms of danger to spite you.

"I know," she said. "Thanks."

I handed her the manuscript. It had started to burn the palms of my hands, like some unholy satanic text.

"I've got a lot of work to catch up on," I told her, also a lie. Then I turned and walked away as nonchalant as I could.

"Sure," she said to my back. Did she stand there and watch me walk away? It felt like she did. But I couldn't turn around and check.

As soon as the front door closed behind me I dropped the act.

"Fuck."

I scrawled Millie's name on the consent form and stuffed it into an envelope, along with her sample. I'd committed felony forgery. (Or was forgery a misdemeanor? God, I hoped so. Was there such a thing as forgery with good intentions?) She was still standing there a minute later when I came flying out of the house and jumped back in the car. She gave a confused look as I sped off towards the post office.

The paternity test promised online results within five business days. That, plus Priority Overnight, and I was looking at about a week.

It was the longest week of my life. I couldn't grade enough papers. I watched *2001* three times (Max had left the tape, the jerk). Each day after work, I raced home to log on to a secure server and check for the results. It technically took five business days, but since I had mailed the package late on a Friday, I didn't have the results until a week from that Monday, a full ten days later.

I rushed into the house just as fast on day ten as I had each day previous. I logged onto the DNA test result website. I cast a nervous glance at the Polaroid of my father and Mrs. Blackford, which I had propped up against the computer, and waited for the page to load. It took forever. When the page finally came up, the screen read:

"RESULTS INCONCLUSIVE BASED ON THE SAMPLES PROVIDED."

Fuck. I immediately dialed customer service. They gave me some bullshit runaround about the quality of the sample. Not Millie's, mine! The guy on the phone gave me a half-hearted sales pitch for some upgraded analysis package that would essentially amount to a more complex explanation of the same result. It would only take an additional ten to twelve business days to process.

Fuck that. I was through fucking around. I had to warn Millie. Hopefully it wasn't too late. I rushed next door.

I was doing a lot of rushing. (*If you choose not to decide you still have made a choice!)* Damn you, Geddy Lee! Why didn't I listen? Canadians are always so level-headed.

TRANSCRIPTION OF CUSTOMER SERVICE PHONE CONVERSATION:

CUSTOMER SERVICE: Hello, my name is [REDACTED]. It is my duty to inform you that our call is being recorded for quality assurance. How may I help you?

ALAN: Yes, I'm calling about my test results.

CS: And what is the transaction number?

[TRANSACTION NUMBER REDACTED]

CS: One moment please… [sound of keys clacking]. It says here that the results were inconclusive.

ALAN: Yes, I know the results were inconclusive, that's why I'm calling.

CS: According to the information I have here, it was due to the quality of the sample provided.

ALAN: We must frequent the same websites. Listen, don't you guys have a more detailed report from the lab or something?

CS: I'm sorry, sir, but that's all the information I'm at liberty to divulge at this time.

ALAN: At liberty to divulge? It's my information!

CS: According to my records, you did not choose our premium service option. For an additional $29.95 I can mail you a notarized copy of our findings, but that would take an additional eight to ten business days.

ALAN: No thank you, that won't be—

CS: Or for $499.99 you could have our expert witnesses testify at your paternity hearing.

[CUSTOMER ABRUPTLY HANGS UP.
END OF TRANSCRIPTION]

THE PARADOX TWINS
by ALBERT LANGLEY

My knuckles pounded on the door rapid fire, so hard they left tiny indentations in the wood. This was no time for the banal playfulness of "Shave and a Haircut." If a percussive equivalent for *open the goddamn door* existed I would have used it.[62]

When Mrs. Blackford answered, I didn't even give her time for one of her patented disdainful hellos. She had to settle for glaring in condescension as I grilled her about Millie's whereabouts. Mrs. Blackford informed me in a calm monotone that Millie had left for a meeting with her editor.

"Her fucking *editor*?"

"Excuse me?"

That got her attention. I sprinted across the lawn back to my car. It sounded like an angry lawnmower as I revved the engine and backed out of the driveway like a maniac.

—

I burst into the pub and headed straight for the booth in the back. Some guy chowing down on nachos had laid claim to it. He looked up, smiled for a split second, then realized which brother I was. A conspicuous copy of *War for Anthropica* sat on the table.

"You know that book's for kids, right?"

I located the waitress who had served us last time we were there, the middle-aged doter who treated Max like the son you know she didn't have.

---

[62] One of the more bombastic compositions by Richard Strauss would have been thematically appropriate.

"Have you seen Max?"

"He left about twenty minutes ago with that cute little number you boys crossed swords over." Her matron's drawl made it sound that much grosser.

"Did he say where they were going?"

"Knowing your brother, he took her back to his hotel room." She gave an unmotherly smile. Bordering on lascivious. She took too much pride in her boy's sexual exploits. I got the hell out of there.

—

Thankfully the lobby of the hotel was empty. No one to embarrass myself in front of. I approached the concierge at a brisk walk, mustering as much authority as I could.

"Excuse me, what room is Max Langley in?"

The effete man behind the counter looked up from the book he perused. Fucking *War For Anthropica*. He had already begun delivering his stock answer as he did so.

"I'm sorry, sir, but we don't give out information about our guests."

His eyes met mine. He had to see the resemblance.

"I'm his twin brother."

Half the concierge's mouth curled up into an amused smirk.

"This isn't my first rodeo, cowboy."

"Excuse me?" Sword fights, rodeos—what the hell was going on tonight?

"You're going to have to try a lot harder than that." The man held up his hand and rubbed his thumb, pointer, and middle finger together in the international sign for "bribe me." Fuck that. I whipped out my license and thrust it in his smug face.

"This isn't a rodeo, dipshit, now which room is my brother in?"

The concierge remained composed, took a step back so he could focus on the license "I'm sorry, but Mr. Langley is with a guest and gave strict orders not to be disturbed."

A guest? What guest? I rattled off a list of questions: Was it a woman? Early twenties? Brown hair? The concierge smirked.

"He does seem to have a type."

Next thing I knew I'd thrown myself over the counter and grabbed the imp by the shirt. Very uncharacteristic words poured out of my mouth.

"Listen to me, you greasy asshat. That girl Max is about to fuck? There's a good chance she's our sister, so you better tell me what room they're in or you'll forever be known as the concierge of the Incest-fucking-Inn."

I shoved and released. *War For Anthropica* went flying. The concierge fell against the wall and slid below the desk, out of sight. A much humbled voice drifted up from behind the wood.

"Room 508."[63]

---

[63] The room became unofficially known as "The Langley Suite" to hotel employees and well-connected patrons after that. The décor is nothing to write home about, but for a fan, the opportunity to occupy the space where such important events took place is priceless. Instead of a Gideons Bible, a copy of *Anthropica* awaits guests in the bedside table.

THE THIRD TWIN
by MILLICENT BLACKFORD

Max behaved like a complete gentleman — at first. He waited until our second meeting to answer his hotel room door in nothing but his socks. Black with yellow paisley.[64] I know this because as soon as I saw him my eyes hit the floor and stayed there for the duration of his nakedness.

Now I know what some of you are thinking. She knew the deal. If she wasn't willing to go through with it she should have never showed up, let alone followed him into that room. And to those people I say, go fuck yourself. You and your high horse. Actually, I hope you get fucked *by* your high horse. A big, strapping stallion. Because until you find yourself embroiled in a similarly imbalanced power dynamic with someone you admire and are willing to give every benefit of the doubt, you have no idea. Hell, if you have a Y chromosome you have no idea.

Anyway, he must have had *some* decency, or at least a few latent confidence issues, because I barreled past him and shamed him into some pants. But not before I slammed my head into the wall trying to navigate the room looking at my shoes. As I sat on the bed rubbing the bump on my forehead, the jolt of pain chased my embarrassment away. And underneath that embarrassment, I was livid.

[64] After the publication of *The Third Twin*, women started showing up at Max's readings wearing yellow paisley socks, pulled up to their knees, in an effort to call him out on his toxic behavior. Max embraced this and soon women began showing up at his readings wearing yellow socks in *support* of him. The whole point of the original protest became muddied and lost.

"What the actual FUCK, Max?"

"I know, I know. Must have gotten my wires crossed. I misread the signals. Totally my fault."

He hopped around on one panted leg, balls flailing, trying to sheath the other. I found it quite comical.

"There's a signal for *Please answer the door with your dick out*? What's semaphore for NO FUCKING WAY?"

He hopped into the bathroom and shut the door. I heard what sounded like a bag of cement hitting the tile, then a winded silence. I used that silence to collect my thoughts. I could picture Alan shaking his head, *I told you so* on the tip of his tongue. The whole mentorship thing was basically fucked, but I thought maybe I could still squeeze an introduction to an agent out of the situation.

Then things went from fucked to farcical. Someone pounded on the hotel room door and Max came flying out of the bathroom, pants on but unbuttoned.

"Hold on a second!" he called as he speed-limped to the door. That fall of his must have been a nasty one.

As he fumbled with the lock I noticed a faded scar along his lower back, like a small, flesh colored tramp stamp. Holy shit—the tail! The one he attributed to Alan in *Breakfast with the Monolith*. If Max hadn't fabricated that part of the story, how much else of it was true? Spacemen visiting from beyond the grave like the Ghost of Christmas Past?

Max pulled the door open a crack and peered out.

"I'm sorry," he said, *sotto voce*, "but could we cancel the champagne?"

The door burst open and bounced off Max's forehead. Alan pushed past him and into the room. I have to admit, I felt relieved to have another person on the scene, but again — things were about to go south.

Alan took in the burgeoning lump on my forehead, his brother's half dressed appearance, saw a conclusion and jumped.

"Millie, are you okay?"

Max sighed and rubbed his own forehead, shut the door behind him.

"I'm fine," I said.

"It's not what it looks like." Max limped back towards the bed. He limped his way right into a fist as Alan wheeled around and punched him square in the jaw. The punch took everyone by surprise, even Alan.

"What the hell was that for?" Max said through a cupped hand.

"That's for trying to fuck our sister!"

"What?!?!" Max and I responded in stereo surprise.

Alan whipped out a Polaroid and threw it at his brother.

"That's Dad and Mrs. Blackford. Guess where I found it?"

Max studied the photo.

"That doesn't prove anything."

Alan snatched the photo back from his brother.

"Doesn't prove anything? You'd take that chance?"

Max shrugged.

"Look, it doesn't matter. Nothing happened."

"I told you to stay away from her!"

"I did! She came to me." Max turned to me for corroboration. "Tell him!"

I opened my mouth to respond, but Alan cut me off.

"She came to you because she thought you were interested in mentoring her career."

 Max laughed.

"What can I say? I'm just a man. I had to make sure."

"You asshole…"

Alan jumped at his brother. They started rolling around on the floor. The photo fluttered to my feet. I picked it up and took a good look.

"This isn't my mother," I said. The fight continued unabated. Put two guys in a room alone with a girl, and if they aren't fighting for her attention, they're fighting each other. I tried again, louder. "*I said*, this isn't my mother."

That did the trick. They stopped mid-grapple to look up at me. Like two lovers caught in a sweaty embrace.

"It's my Aunt."

Max pushed Alan away from him.

"There, you see? No harm, no foul. Dad wasn't boning Mrs. Blackford, it was her sister."

"Shut the fuck up." Alan walked over to get a better look. "Are you sure?"

"Positive," I said. "She died when I was a baby. Mom talks about her all the time. I'm her namesake."

Alan sat next to me on the bed, tried to catch his breath. His protectiveness made a little more sense now. A rush of emotion swelled within my chest.

"You thought I was your sister?"

Alan shrugged.

"A little, yeah."

"That's sweet."

I could hear Max's eyes roll.

"Very slick, Albert. If I'd known that's all I had to do, I would have shown her that picture weeks ago."

I was prepared to let the comment go, as one must often do when one is a woman, but Alan latched onto it. He was right to, but I kind of wish he hadn't.

"What did you say?"

Max backpedaled.

"I mean, you know, had I known about it."[65]

Holy shit, he knew. Bile rose to oppose the warm feeling in my chest. Hippocratic humors waged war inside me.

"You knew, didn't you?" Alan continued.

"Come on, Al, don't be ridiculous…"

"You fucking knew. It was near the top of the the pile, you had to have seen it…and you were going to anyway."

We all knew what "going to" meant. Alan got up and advanced on Max. Max backed away, tried to get to his feet.

"Even if I did see it, what were the odds? Besides, that would have only made her our half-sister."

"I can't believe this. You're worse than Dad."

"Oh, fuck you. You would have done the exact same thing. That's what all this Knight in Shining Armor bullshit is about."

"You're wrong. That's not what this is about, and I'm nothing like you."

"Yes you are. We're twins. We're practically the same person. You're just afraid to admit it."

---

[65] Once a liar, always a liar. They're like alcoholics that way. In a constant state of recovery.

Alan paused, looked in my direction for support. I gave him my most neutral look. It wasn't what he wanted.

"The fuck I am."

Alan attacked Max with even more violence than before. I screamed for them to stop to no avail. They rolled around the room, crashing into walls and knocking over furniture. I stood up on the bed to stay out of harm's way. Despite my perch I had to do plenty of evasive maneuvering. The phrase *boys will be boys* floated through my head. Except I replaced the word *boys* with *assholes*.

Things continued to escalate. Alan had his hands around Max's throat. Max pushed his brother off him, sending him reeling. Alan stumbled backwards and tripped on an over-turned chair. His head came down on the sharp corner of the nightstand. Hard. The space between furniture and man blossomed red. I screamed as he hit the floor.

"Alan!"

Max jumped to his feet.

"Shit! Albert!"

Alan tried to get up, but couldn't maintain his balance. He babbled incoherently, a trail of spittle trickling down the side of his mouth. I jumped off the bed and tried to calm him. I turned to Max.

"Call an ambulance!"

Alan's eyes rolled into the back of his head. Blood slicked his hair and shirt. I led him over to the bed, tried to get him to lay down. Max grabbed the phone and dialed the front desk.

"We need an ambulance to room 508, immediately."

Alan continued to struggle. Max got on the other side of him and helped me hold him down. Alan fought against us, but soon expended his remaining energy. His body shook as he went into seizure. Max laid across him like a weighted blanket. We almost had him under control when he opened his mouth and let out the most blood-curdling scream I'd ever heard. Not one of pain, but of madness. The sound of a man watching his mind slip away knowing he couldn't do anything about it. (Sorry, Alan. Taking a little poetic license, I know. But it scared me that much.)

Alan had passed out by the time the paramedics arrived. They loaded him onto a gurney and wheeled him towards the elevator, a little too nonchalant for my tastes. The ambulance only had room for one, so I hopped in and Max followed in his BMW. Apparently he got a sweet rental in addition to unlimited access to limos. (I'm not being petty, just noting for continuity.)

My hand still clutched the Polaroid picture. I can't believe Aunt Millie and Mr. Langley... Had Alan really thought I was his half-sister? The idea of having anything remotely close to a sibling choked me up. I was kind of disappointed it wasn't mom in the picture. At least then I would have known who my father was. The paramedic did me the courtesy of averting his eyes as I cried. [66]

---

[66] In light of this scene, I suppose it's understandable that Millie has been hesitant to allow fans access to her inner circle, especially male fans. Although I think it's unfair to call her demeanor at signings "standoffish." I'm sure it's a head-trip to have several hundred people clamoring for your attention. The amount of time it takes to scribble a signature is hardly enough to make an impression, let alone share some sort of meaningful connection. Also not recommended: accosting your favorite author on the street. Trust me, most of them don't like surprises. Like the time that guy followed Millie home from one of her readings wearing a red spacesuit.

BREAKFAST WITH THE MONOLITH – LARRY BRIGHT – 10/11/13 DRAFT

INT. AMBULANCE – NIGHT[67]

CLOSE-UP, HEAVY ON THE DUTCH – A foot stomps on the gas, PEDAL to the METAL.

                              SMASH CUT TO:

A SPINNING TIRE

EXT. STREET – NIGHT

TIRES SQUEAL and RUBBER BURNS as the ambulance peels out and launches down the road, SIRENS FLASHING.

Seconds later, Max's RED FERRARI comes flying out of the hotel parking lot, in HOT PURSUIT. The fiberglass beast fishtails, kicking up dust as it jumps the curb and takes the corner.

---

[67] I find the awfulness of this whole sequence fascinating. *ER* meets *The Fast and the Furious.*

INT. AMBULANCE - NIGHT

Millie tries to make herself as small as possible while the EMTs work. Supplies emblazoned with the logos of BIG PHARMA fill the shelves, a sickening reminder of the over-monetization of human life.

NOTE: If this becomes a product placement issue, use BITING CORPORATE PARODIES such as NO-ARTISTS, DSPIZER, and MERC (as in MERCENARY. A play on MERCK. Too subtle?)

A stoic EMT #1, young but already hardened by the job, grabs the CB with a rubber-gloved hand.

                    EMT #1
    Inbound with a 45 year old male.
    Blunt force trauma to the head.
    Superficial bleeding, possible
    epidural hematoma. ETA six minutes.

EXT. STREET - NIGHT

The ambulance speeds through a yellow light. HORNS BLARE as Max follows, blows the red, swerves to barely miss oncoming traffic. An angry driver extends his fist out his window and shakes it.

INT. FERRARI - NIGHT

Max flips the bird in the rearview mirror, his middle digit protruding from a fingerless, mesh racing glove.

INT. AMBULANCE - NIGHT

The contents of the ambulance swing back and forth as Millie fights to maintain her balance. The heroic EMTs seem unfazed. BUSINESS AS USUAL. A high-pitched ALARM sounds.

>   MILLIE
> What's happening?

>   EMT #2
> He's going into cardiac arrest.
>   (To EMT #1)
> Clear the airway and prep for CPR.

EMT #1 snakes a suction catheter down Alan's throat.

> EMT #1
>
> Passage clear!

EMT #1 whips out the tube, mucus dripping from its tip.

> EMT #2
>
> Oxygenating.

EMT #2 places an oxygenation mask over Alan's mouth, squeezes the rubber bulb. He alternates this activity with EMT #1, who compresses Alan's chest. Neither has broken a sweat.

EXT. STREET - NIGHT

The ambulance takes another hard corner. It hits a bottomless pit of a POTHOLE, which sends a GLEAMING HUBCAP spinning down the street.

It rolls past a scraggly HOMELESS MAN in an army jacket--A VETERAN--briefly reflecting his face as he watches it pass. HIS FACE is OUR FACE, a nation culpable for his predicament. But does he feel sorry for himself? No.

He salutes the vehicle as it passes,
a single tear in his eye.

                HOMELESS VETERAN
    Godspeed, heroes.

INT. AMBULANCE - NIGHT

EMT #2 removes the oxygenation mask
and glances at the monitor.

                EMT #2
    He's not responding. Initiate
    defib.

Millie looks on as EMT #2 squirts
a healthy dollop of electrode gel
on one of the paddles and smears it
between the two. EMT #1 mans the
defibrillator.

                EMT #2
    Charge for 360.

                EMT #1
    Charging.

                    EMT #2
        All clear?

EMT #2 places the paddles on the
upper right and lower left chest
walls.

                    EMT #1
        Shocking.

Alan's lifeless body jumps, prompting
Millie to jump as well.

EXT. HOSPITAL - NIGHT

The ambulance pulls up in front of
the hospital and slams on the brakes.
Max follows in the Ferrari, FISH-
TAILING side to side as he swerves to
avoid the ambulance. He leaves the
car running and hops out.

Max and Millie watch as the EMTs
unload Alan and wheel him into the
emergency entrance.

INT. HOSPITAL - CONTINUOUS

HANDHELD: Max and Millie follow the gurney inside. DOCTOR BENNET meets the EMTs. They all take part in a classic RUN AND GUN hospital admission scene.

                    DOCTOR BENNET
          What do we have?

                    EMT #2
          Head trauma. Possible swelling.
          Went code blue on the way in.

                    DOCTOR BENNET
          Alright, get him prepped and into
          OR three.

The EMTs wheel Alan off. Max and Millie go to follow. Doctor Bennet stops them.

                    DOCTOR BENNET
          I'm sorry, but you'll have to
          remain in the waiting area.

                    MILLIE
          Is he going to be okay?

DOCTOR BENNET

He's sustained a serious injury, but it doesn't appear to be life threatening. We'll inform you as soon as we know more.

THE THIRD TWIN
by MILLICENT BLACKFORD

Max and I sat in the waiting room in uncomfortable silence. Uncomfortable for me, at least, especially since I was about to start grilling him again. Who knows what was going on inside that self-centered brain of his. Probably working out how Alan's injury would fit into the larger narrative of his work in progress.

Which got me thinking about my own place in the Langley saga. Everything had happened so fast, only now did I have time to start processing events. For a moment there, I had almost been one of them.

"Did you really know?" I asked Max. "About the picture?"

He opened his mouth to speak. Closed it. Opened it again. I saw resignation in his eyes."Yeah," he said, voice barely audible.

"This isn't a library," I admonished him. "You don't have to whisper."

"I said YES."

He met my eyes as he repeated the word, defiant. I felt hurt, angry, confused—I didn't want this to be easy for him. We stared at each other in silence, embroiled in a contest of will. I continued to deny my culpability for what had happened. Was this whole thing my fault? If I hadn't gotten myself into this mess, Alan wouldn't have had to come to my rescue. My stubbornness had turned me into the character I hated most—the Damsel in Distress.[68] My thoughts teetered on the precipice of a shame spiral. Thankfully the doctor interrupted them.

"Mr. Langley?"

I jumped to my feet, positioning myself between Max and the doctor.

"How is he?"

The doctor looked back and forth between us, sensing something he did not want to be a part of.

"His condition is stable," the doctor said. "The force of the trauma caused some swelling on the brain, but it's under control now. If we can keep the swelling down, we shouldn't have to operate."

Max poked his head out from behind me.

"Can we see him?"

I stepped in front of him again, so the doctor had no choice but to continue addressing me.

"Only for a minute. He won't regain consciousness for a few more hours. I don't want him disturbed before then."

Down the corridor we went. The doctor held the door open and we filed into the room. Alan's pallor matched the bandage wrapped around his head. Tubes and wires ran in and out of his body. Max's face fell when he saw him.

"This is fucked," he said.

I turned to Max, doing my best not to cry.

---

[68] I know modern women don't appreciate being rescued, but what happens when a woman needs to be rescued from herself? It's like involuntarily committing a psych patient—sometimes it has to be done. I mean, it should have never happened to me, but in some cases, it's the right thing to do.

"Is that all you have to say?"

He shrugged.

"What do you want to hear?"

I thought about it. I didn't have an answer, so I said the obvious.

"How about an apology?"

Max gestured towards his brother.

"It's not like he can hear me."

I couldn't tell if he was trying to be funny or not. His cavalier attitude grated on my nerves.

"He's not the only one in the room," I shot back.

Max made eye contact for the second time since we arrived at the hospital. This time it felt like less of a face off. It almost felt human.

"Look, I know there are a lot of things that need to be said, but I can't right now." I held his gaze for what I considered an appropriate amount of time, showing neither weakness nor combativeness, then I turned back to Alan.

"He's right, you know," I said to Max. "You guys are two totally different people."

Max didn't take the bait. He knew better than to open that can of worms.

"Why don't you go home, get some rest?" he said. "I'll give you a call when he's awake."

It felt like a dismissal, but I was too exhausted to argue. If he wanted to do this on his own, so be it. I turned to go.

"Could you do me one favor?"

There it was. I prepared myself for a demeaning request, some final indignity so he could maintain the illusion of having the upper hand. Could I bring him a fresh pair of underwear, or something equally ridiculous. I turned to glare at Max.

"What?" I said, a little too harshly. That's when I noticed he wasn't looking at me. He stood over his brother, searching his face for signs of life. Maybe he saw himself reflected back.

"Could you grab the picture of me and Al from the house? The one on the mantel?"

I went soft inside.

"Sure."

BREAKFAST WITH THE MONOLITH - JAGER CARTWRIGHT - 7/9/15 DRAFT

INT. HOSPITAL ROOM - NIGHT

Max sits by his unconscious brother, staring at the tubes running in and out of his body.

> MAX
> I really cocked things up good, didn't I?

He pauses, as if expecting a response.

> MAX (CONT'D)
> I mean, you did hit me first, but I guess I sort of deserved it. Payback for all the times I wailed on you, right? If only Dad could see us now.

Max shifts his weight, leans in close.

> MAX (CONT'D)
> (sotto voice)
> You're not with him now, are you? Because I'd love to ask him a few questions. You know, for the book.

Alan grunts in his sleep. Max leans back in his chair.

> MAX (CONT'D)
>
> I'm kidding. The story's actually become a lot bigger than Dad. I'm having a bit of trouble with the climax, though. Maybe you could help? This has never happened to me before, I swear.

Max leaves a beat for non-existent laughter.

> MAX (CONT'D)
>
> You see, I can't tell if the story should have a down-beat ending or not. Does the brother wake up from his coma? And if he does, will things ever be the same? I don't know which way things are going to shake out. What do you think?

Max lets the question hang, waiting for a response that never comes.

INT. LANGLEY HOUSE - NIGHT

Millie lets herself in and flips on the
lights. An unnatural QUIET dominates the--

LIVING ROOM

She walks over to the mantle and
picks up the framed photo of Max
and Alan. Studies it. The toy rocket
obscures one of their faces. Which
twin is which?

She puts the frame inside her bag and
continues to walk around the room,
taking in the details. She picks
things up. Puts them down.

She sits down on the couch, the first
moment she's had to rest since everything happened. That's when the tears
come.

She gets it out of her system. Sighs.
Leans back against the couch and closes
her eyes. She starts to drift, when—

The sound of FOOTSTEPS brings her back
to attention.

                    MILLIE
        Hello?

Her breath comes out in a white cloud
of condensation. When did it get so
cold in here? She hugs herself and
listens with intent. Nothing.

She gets up, is about to leave when
she hears it again. The footsteps
sound like they come from upstairs.

                    MILLIE
        Is someone there?

But the house is once again silent.
She climbs the stairs towards the sound.

INT. PAUL'S ROOM - CONTINUOUS

Millie hovers in the doorway,shivering.
She peers into the shadows. Is that
movement? She reaches a hand into the
room, flips the light switch.

There is no one there.

She sees a physics textbook and a
paperback copy of "2001: A SPACE

ODYSSEY" by Arthur C. Clarke on the bedstand. Millie blows warm air into her fist and flips through the textbook. A piece of paper with handwritten notes and formulas bookmarks a section on the Twins Paradox.

She puts down the textbook and picks up the tattered paperback.

She is startled by a NOISE from across the house, louder than the previous one. Like someone rummaging. She tucks the book under her arm and goes to investigate.

INT. LANGLEY HOUSE - CONTINUOUS

Millie traverses the house on tip-toes, each breath a puff of white.

> MILLIE
> Is there anyone there? I can hear you.

She approaches the door of the study, which swings ajar. The sound of RUSTLING PAPERS can be heard from within. She knocks.

                    MILLIE
       Hello?

She grips the knob. Pushes…

INT. STUDY - CONTINUOUS

The door swings open, revealing
Millie's silhouette. She reaches
for the light switch. She flips it.
Screams.

A raccoon perches on the desk. Loose
papers flutter to the ground, scattered by the breeze from an open
window. The animal leaps from the
desk to the window sill, then disap-
pears into the night.

Millie crosses the study and slams
the window shut. She leans against it
to catch her breath.

She kneels down to gather up the
papers. They are all related to Paul
Langley's life and work. She comes
across a newspaper clipping. The
headline reads:

"LOCAL PROF ACCUSED OF IMPROPRIETY"

She picks up another one:

"PREGNANT STUDENT SEEKS RESTITUTION
FROM HER PROFESSOR"

                    MILLIE
     Pregnant?

She pulls the Polaroid of her Aunt
from her bag and studies it.[69]

---

[69] I love this whole sequence. Oscar caliber monologue, edge-of-your-seat suspense, and a fantastic reveal to cap it off. The 7/9/15 Jager Cartwright draft of the *Breakfast with the Monolith* screenplay is by far the best. Give that guy more work. Seriously.

BOSTON HERALD

LOCAL PROF SUES UNIVERSITY FOR UNLAWFUL TERMINATION OVER SEXUAL IMPROPRIETY

CAMBRIDGE, MA — The M.I.T. professor fired for having a consensual affair with one of his students has filed suit against the University for unlawful termination.

Paul Langley, noted physicist and PhD, filed suit Tuesday morning, foregoing his previous anonymity in the matter.

The school chancellor first acknowledged the dismissal in his weekly email to the campus community. The unidentified undergraduate involved in the affair reported the impropriety herself after the professor put an end to the relationship. She claims he did so after she informed him of her pregnancy.

The student is said to have received supervision and course counselling from the faculty member throughout the relationship, a direct violation of the Faculty Code of Conduct. A review of the case by the Board of Trustees upheld the decision to terminate.

University Administration declined to comment on the lawsuit.

Mr. Langley is represented by the private practice of Todd Barnett, Esq.

THE THIRD TWIN
by MILLICENT BLACKFORD

Against my better judgment I retrieved the photograph for Max. I told myself I did it for Alan's sake. Although, if I woke up from a coma and saw the guy who put me there brandishing a framed photo that represented everything wrong with our relationship, I'd do one of three things: punch him in the face, shit myself with rage, or pass the fuck back out.

The old Langley place (I make it sound like something out of a Scooby Doo cartoon) was pretty spooky at night. Alan and Max had done a great job cleaning up, and the current sparseness gave the impression of a home unlived in. Only the few personal items left, like the framed photograph, gave it any character. I contemplated snooping around a bit, but decided against it. I wanted to spend as little time alone there as possible. The place had too many figurative ghosts. And according to Alan, some literal ones as well.

Mom was waiting for me when I got home. I flicked on the lights and there she was, sitting in her rocking chair. I nearly jumped out of my skin. Old people in rocking chairs are inherently creepy—even if they're related to you. I would have expected a jump scare at the Langley's place, not here in my own home.

"Jeez, Mom, you scared the crap out of me." I still didn't like cursing in front of my mother. "What are you doing sitting alone in the dark like that?"

The rocking chair creaked as my mother's toes met the floor and pushed off again. "Couldn't sleep. How'd the meeting go?"

"Meeting?" So much had happened since my quote unquote meeting, I'd forgotten all about it. My mother raised an eyebrow while I searched the old memory banks.

"With Max?" she offered, jogging my memory.

"Oh, that meeting... not so good, actually."

Mom nodded, which in her world equated to saying "I told you so." Apparently she'd put a name to my faceless editor.

"Alan came here looking for you earlier," she said. "It seemed... important."

"Did you tell him where I went?" I already had a good idea of the answer.

"I told him what I knew, which wasn't much."

We lapsed into silence. I had no idea where to take the conversation. Were we going to talk about Dad? We were going to talk about Dad. It'd been so long. I didn't know if I could handle the conversation. But in light of the evening's developments...

"I'm worried about you," Mom said. "Want to tell me what's going on?"

"I came from the hospital. Alan hit his head. We had to call an ambulance."

Mom processed what I'd said. I could see her playing all the angles. I hadn't lied to her, but she could tell I was doling out information piece by need-to-know piece.

"And how is he?"

"He's stable. They're still waiting for him to wake up. Max is gonna call me as soon as he does."

THE PARADOX TWINS   213

"How did it happened?"

"The two of them had a fight."

Mom blinked. Once. Twice...

"Over me... I think."

She nodded her head. Not an I-told-you-so nod, more an acknowledgement she was satisfied I'd told her the truth. That allowed her to move on to her secondary concern.

"And what about you? Are you okay?"

I sat down across from my mother, in the chair that had been strategically placed for me, for this very conversation. I took a deep breath. Time to lay my cards on the table. I promised myself that if she didn't answer my questions, if I couldn't give a satisfied little nod indicating she had told me what I wanted to know, we would never have this conversation again. Hell, we might never have *any* conversation again.

"There's something I need to ask you." I left a nice little pregnant pause, tried to gauge her reaction. *Pregnant.* Such an appropriate word. I felt like our whole relationship had been one big pregnant pause. A pause Mom seemed plenty comfortable with, while I teetered on eggshells around her.

"Did Aunt Millie and Mr. Langley... you know."

She tilted her head. I could tell it wasn't a question she'd expected.

"Where did you hear that?"

I handed her the Polaroid.

"Do I have a cousin you never told me about?"

She studied the incriminating photo in silence. Was that moisture welling up in her eyes? A crack in her stony facade? I held my breath and waited. Finally, Mom let loose a big, wet sob that wracked her entire body. I immediately started to cry.

"It's…" Mom ran a finger along the photograph, as if she could touch her sister's face. Then she looked up and met my eyes, and yes, there were tears there. Tears that had been a long time coming, held behind a dam of stoicism. They also contained years of pent up compassion, misguided though it might have been.

"It's not what you think," she said.

A combination of impatience and fear flooded my system. I'd been desperate for answers about my family my whole life. Now, on the verge of getting what I always wanted, I was getting cold feet. I pulled my chair closer and took her hand.

And then she told me everything.

—

I let the hot water mingle with the tears that continued to fall. A soothing combination that cleansed the emotion being expunged from my body. By the time I'd stepped out of the shower I was all cried out.

I wrapped a towel around myself and wiped a hand across the fogged bathroom mirror. The clear streak exposed a pink, puffy face. I looked terrible. What a way to end the day.

I grabbed a brush and started working it through my tangles. My absent-minded gaze drifted towards the window, towards the Langley house. I found myself staring at the spot on the lawn where I'd found Mr. Langley. How long had he been standing there, I wondered? Had he known it was his time?

I remembered finding Alan in that exact same spot, heart jumping into my throat. At the time I thought, oh no, not again. After years of not following in his father's footsteps, it looked like he had finally decided to start. Part of me wanted to go down there and stand on that spot, see if I could see what he had been looking at. What he'd been reaching for.

Instead I got into bed with my copy of *War For Anthropica*. Now that I'd gotten to know the Langley's better, my second read through was proving to be especially enlightening. I opened to Max's inscription and stopped. That's all I had the stomach for. I leaned back and closed my eyes, tried to think about what to tell Max and Alan the next time I saw them. If I should tell them Mom's secret or not.

BREAKFAST WITH THE MONOLITH - LUCAS ATIMA - 12/16/14 DRAFT

INT. MILLIE'S ROOM - NIGHT

Millie picks up the copy of "2001" she got from the Langley house. She opens to the forward, sees a high-lighted line:

"Behind every man now alive stands a ghost"[70]

She turns the page. Further down, another highlighted phrase:

"...one day we shall meet our equals, or our masters, among the stars."

INT. BLACKFORD HOUSE - NIGHT

Mrs. Blackford sits in the dark, staring at the Polaroid Millie gave her. She opens a PHOTO ALBUM. Pictures of her and her sister.

---

[70] A mistake? Or a liberty taken by the writer? The actual quote being: *Behind every man now alive stand thirty ghosts*, a reference to the ratio by which the dead outnumbered the living (at the time). 29 too many ghosts for the purposes of our story.

She turns the page. More family photos. Finally: A picture of Mrs. Blackford and a noticeably pregnant Aunt Millie. She slips the Polaroid behind it.

INT. MILLIE'S ROOM - NIGHT

Millie sleeps, book on her chest. The Spaceman stands at the foot of her bed, watching her.

INT. HOSPITAL ROOM - NIGHT

Alan sleeps. His eyelids twitch. Max sleeps in the chair next to him.

INT. MILLIE'S ROOM - NIGHT

The Spaceman takes slow strides towards the side of the bed.

INT. HOSPITAL ROOM - NIGHT

Perspiration beads on Alan's forehead.

INT. MILLIE'S ROOM - NIGHT

The Spaceman reaches out for Millie's face. As it touches her--

INT. HOSPITAL ROOM - NIGHT

--Alan opens his eyes.

INT. MILLIE'S ROOM - NIGHT

Millie's cell phone rings. She snaps awake and grabs it.

                    MILLIE
          Hello? I'll be right there.

She jumps out of bed, begins to get dressed, pauses. She looks towards the foot of her bed, but there is nothing there.

THE PARADOX TWINS
by ALBERT LANGLEY

Memory is a funny thing. Max was never one for remembering details that didn't pertain to him. Names only stuck if they were attached to a pretty face or someone who could further his career. Growing up he never once remembered a family member's birthday, yet he could quote Asimov's Three Laws of Robotics verbatim. Hell, sometimes he forgot *my* birthday, and it's the same damn day as his.

Me, I've always been good with names and numbers, but thanks to a little thing called retrograde amnesia I have almost no recollection of what happened after I stormed into Max's hotel room that fateful day. I don't know who said what to whom, yet any time I press my cheek against a hotel room carpet it triggers a disorienting wave of nausea. A sort of haptic response that has instilled in me a preference for hardwood floors.

Head injuries are nothing like what you see in movies and TV. That trope where a guy gets whacked on the back of the head with a sock full of quarters then wakes up in another location, groggy but generally no worse for wear? That is some grade-A bullshit. Nothing but a convenient scene break. A way to get a character from point A to point B with minimal storytelling. They never tell you about the ignominy of pissing yourself or involuntarily voiding your bowels. It doesn't take a whole lot of blunt force to cause cranial bleeding or even seizure, and a well placed blow can cause permanent damage to motor functions. Lucky for me I've seemed to escape the clutches of any long term effects.

My first recollection post-accident was of Max talking to himself. Well, actually, he was talking to me, but he was saying things he'd never say if he knew I was listening. Featured heavily were phrases like "you were right" and "I'm sorry." Come to think of it, maybe I hallucinated the whole thing. That would make much more sense.

Either way, I let him ramble, hoping he'd stumble upon an epiphany. I continued to feign sleep, on the verge of drifting off again, when I heard Millie enter the room. Max offered her his seat like a true gentleman and she pulled it over to the bed. I allowed my eyes to flutter open. A worried smile greeted me as Millie's blurry face filled my field of vision.

"How do you feel?" she asked.

I felt like shit, but forced a smile. It came out crooked.

"You scared me."

Max nudged Millie in the back.

"Us," she said. "You scared us."

"Sorry." The word hurt coming up. Millie took my hand in hers, tears pooling below her eyes. Max, in an unprecedented show of awareness, turned to leave.

"I'll let you two talk."

"No, wait," Millie said. Max paused mid-step, as desperate to be included as ever. "There's something I need to tell you guys."

Max and I exchanged looks. Millie waited for him to retrace his steps and rejoin our little campfire circle before continuing. Whatever she had to say, it was going to be big.

"Remember when I said that Polaroid wasn't of my mom? That it was my Aunt?" She paused to take a breath, a well placed beat. The question hung in the air and we hung on her every word. A technique she must have picked up from watching Max on stage. "I was wrong. Kind of."

We were stunned. I know I was. The look on his face said Max was too. My throat hurt too much, so I let him ask the questions I knew he would.

"What do you mean? How do you know?"

Millie hung her head, as if admitting a shameful secret.

"My mother told me. I mean, my aunt. Basically, my mother is my aunt and my aunt is my mother. It's confusing."

But it wasn't. I knew exactly what she meant. Why hadn't I seen it? I could tell Max was almost there as well, he just needed a little help across the finish line.

"So does that mean...?"

Millie nodded her head.

"Paul Langley was my father. Aunt Millie, the woman in the picture, was my real mom."[71]

Max took a step back and put a hand over his mouth. Either to silence himself or hide his reaction. Me, I could barely move, so I let my eyes do my emoting for me. Millie continued.

"She ran off after I was born, and my mom—my aunt, really—raised me as her own."

Millie looked deep into my eyes. All I could do was look back.

---

[71] Initially Max wanted to use the photo of his father and Millie's mother for the cover of *BwtM*, but both Alan and Millie objected and threatened legal action, so a reproduction was used instead.

"The student Mr. Langley got fired for having an affair with? That was Millicent Blackford. My mother."

Max put his hands on Millie's shoulders. She shrugged them off.

"Don't. I'm still trying to process the whole thing."

An uncomfortable silence followed, interrupted only by the periodic beeping of my heart monitor. Max didn't let it last long, however, and for once, I was grateful. Until I heard what he had to say, that is.

"Did you bring the picture?"

He had the worst sense of timing. Did he have to see it again right now? But when Millie reached into her bag, she didn't come out with the Polaroid like I expected. She handed Max the framed photo from the mantle. The one of us in the sandbox, fighting over the toy rocket. Max studied it.

"Remember that night we talked about the Twins Paradox?" He didn't wait for an answer. Even incapable of speech, he knew it'd be the last thing I'd want to talk about. "Thing is, it's not actually a paradox at all. Special relativity doesn't claim all observers are equivalent, only those at rest in inertial reference frames. The twin traveling in the spaceship jumps frames when he turns his ship around. It's during this period of acceleration that the two observers are not equivalent, thus the difference in age does not constitute a contradiction of logic."

Millie gave a blank stare. I begrudgingly nodded in the affirmative.

"But that's assuming the twins aren't equivalent. If you take special relativity out of the equation, and there are no shifts in the reference frame, that's where a paradox would occur, because both twins would view the other as traveling, therefore each would appear to the other as having aged slower."

"Wait a minute," Millie interrupted. "I thought you said your father used the Twins Paradox as an allegory to pit you guys against each other."

"There's more to it than that," Max said. "It's a role, one I've been playing my whole life." He pointed to the picture. "You see this? Alan's the twin with the rocket ship, not me. I switched around details in my manuscript to make myself look better. He was born first. I'm the one who was born with a tail, not him."

"I saw the scar, remember?" Millie said, annoyed. "What difference does it make?"

"It makes a difference to me. And I bet it does to my brother, too. I guess what I'm trying to say is, I'm not the one who's out of this world. Scientifically speaking, from my frame of reference, Alan is."

Millie turned away from Max to look at me. Footsteps echoed from out in the hallway.

"Okay, I still don't get it," she said. "Was that an apology?"

As much as it hurt, I couldn't help but smile. I looked over at Max.

"A big one," I said.

And that's how the doctor found us, grinning like idiots. If I didn't know any better, I'd say he had the timing of a writer, too.

"Alright, I think that's enough excitement for one day. Let's let the patient get some rest."

Max placed the framed photo on the bedside table, reached over and squeezed my shoulder. The doctor let us have our moment before ushering Max and Millie out into the hall. I closed my eyes to think about everything I'd heard. Millie's revelation. Max's apology. I felt a warm, tingly sensation at the top of my skull. That sensation ran down my face, like an invisible egg had been cracked on my head. It continued down my entire body, across my chest and down my limbs. It felt nice. I smiled as it enveloped my body.

And that's the last thing I remember.

INT. HALLWAY - CONTINUOUS

Max and Millie stand outside Alan's
room in awkward silence. Max looks
around the hallway, tries to find the
words. Millie stares at her feet.

> MAX
> Look, I'm sorry for being such a
> scumbag.

> MILLIE
> For the record, you were pretty
> scummy.

> MAX
> As you can already tell, being a
> Langley is not without its
> difficulties.

> MILLIE
> No, it's not.

More silence.

                    MAX
          Half-siblings, huh?

                    MILLIE
                 (nodding)
          Yep.

Millie looks up to meet his eyes. Max
smiles, extends his arms for a hug.

                    MAX
          Welcome to the family.

Max takes a step forward. Millie
takes a step back.

                    MILLIE
          Easy. It's gonna take me a while
          to get over the whole you-trying-
          to-sleep-with-me thing.

                    MAX
          Right.

Millie extends a hand. The two shake.

An ALARM sounds from inside Alan's room.

INT. HOSPITAL ROOM - CONTINUOUS

Max and Millie rush in. Alan con-
vulses on the bed. Millie looks to
Max. He runs to the door.

MAX
Nurse? Nurse!

BREAKFAST WITH THE MONOLITH
by MAX LANGLEY

THE STARGATE SEQUENCE: JUPITER AND BEYOND THE INFINITE

Max and Millie stand outside Alan's hospital room sharing an awkward silence. Like bar patrons who have been told they don't have to go home, but continuing to occupy their current location is no longer an option. Wandering eyes scan the hallway as brains search for the appropriate words. Max stumbles upon them first.

"Look, I'm sorry for being such a scumbag."

Millie—arms crossed, right foot tap-tap-tapping—acknowledges this admission with a slight nod of the head.

"For the record, you *were* pretty scummy. I'd go so far as calling you the *lord* of scum."

Max gives a non-threatening version of his famous grin. The grin that launched a thousand ships, ships invariably dashed against rocks floating through space.

"As you can already tell, being a Langley is not without its difficulties."

"It certainly isn't."

The well of words dries up and silence resumes. But actions speak louder than words. Max spreads his arms wide for a hug.

"Am I forgiven?"

He's a scoundrel, but a lovable one. It only takes Millie a fraction of a second to consider.

"Sure." She steps into the hug and puts her head against his chest. Max closes his arms around her. He's the closest thing she has to a father.[72] He's also the best shot she has at getting published. "As long as you promise to introduce me to your editor," she says.

Max's famous grin widens until it fills the corridor.

"Welcome to the family, sis. You're gonna fit in fine."

The blare of an alarm interrupts this touching scene. Millie and Max jump apart, as if caught in an illicit moment. They scan the hallway for the source of the offending sound. It doesn't take long to realize it comes from Alan's room.

Max and Millie rush in to find Alan mid convulsion. His eyes have rolled into the back of his head, his jaw clenched tight. Millie looks to Max for guidance, unsure of what to do. Max sticks his head into the hallway and yells for the nurse. She rushes in to check the monitors.

"What happened?" the nurse demands, as if they've done something wrong. She taps the screen of the Heart and Lung 9000. The angry red eye of its power indicator stares, unblinking. "We were out in the hall and he started freaking out." Tears well up in Millie's eyes.

The young nurse yanks the phone from its cradle.

"Doctor Barratt to room 237[73] immediately. Repeat, Doctor Barratt to room 237."

All the while Alan's body continues to shake beneath the sheets.

---

[72] Really, the closest thing she has to a brother—a half-brother.

[73] Newton-Wellesley Hospital has no room 237.

On the inside of his eyelids, visible to only him, colors pulsate and change, bleeding into one another.

Doctor Barratt rushes in, checks the machines, and barks orders at the nurse.

"What the hell's going on?" Max asks. "I thought he was stable?" The doctor, gentle but firm, moves Max out of the way, saying nothing.

Bright colors accelerate towards Alan from a fixed point in the distance. The alarms and yelling in the hospital room sound muffled and far away to his ears.

"Blood pressure's dropping. We need to reduce the swelling on his brain." Doctor Barratt whips out a penlight, pulls open an eyelid, and shines it into Alan's yawning pupil.

The brief flash creates a mirror effect. The reflection passes through the vitreous and hits the retina, superimposing an image of his own iris over the rush of color he experiences.

"Alan? Alan?" A voice keeps repeating his name, but he hardly hears it. The spike of light ends and Alan's eyelid snaps shut. The sounds of the hospital room fade away and are replaced by the roar of acceleration. Streaks of color shoot past, recede into the periphery. Then stars and planets, followed by solar systems and galaxies. Positive and negative space are inverted, creating something out of nothing and nothing out of something. The colors bleed due to the g-force, streaming away in rivulets like rain against the windshield of a moving vehicle. Once the color has completely drained away, nothing remains but all encompassing black. A darkness more vast than the universe. An endless void.

When he opens his eyes again, he finds the hospital room

silent and empty. No doctors, no nurses, no Millie, no Max. The machines have ceased their beeping. The only other entity present is the man-sized black monolith standing at the foot of the bed. No fugue of howling wind emanates from within. There is a complete and total lack of sound. Not even room tone to orient the inner-ear. A vacuum, louder than any silence.

Alan blinks and the scene changes to a more familiar one. He is back in his father's house, lying in his father's bed. The monolith has followed and continues to loom over him. Alan cowers in its shadow.

He blinks and finds himself back in the empty hospital room. The monolith has been replaced by a figure in a red spacesuit with silver trim, an orange panel strapped to its chest. Alan blinks yet again and he is back in his father's room, the Spaceman standing at the foot of the bed.

"Dad?" he says, voice small like a child's. The Spaceman turns and retreats down the hallway. Alan gets out of bed to follow.

He trails the Spaceman through the house. The Spaceman takes giant steps across the living room, shifting his weight from one leg to the other as if walking across the surface of the moon. As he passes the mantle he knocks over the framed photo of the twins in the sandbox. Alan picks up the picture. A huge crack cuts across the glass, splitting the image in two.

Meanwhile, Max and Millie attempt to stay out of the way as Doctor Barratt and the nurses rush to stabilize Alan. One of them bumps into the framed photo on the bedside table. It falls to the ground, and a huge crack streaks across the glass.

Alan walks out onto the front lawn. The Spaceman stands in the spot where Paul Langley died, looking up at the bright white dot of Jupiter. Alan closes the distance between them with caution. He reaches out and places a hand on the Spaceman's shoulder.

Simultaneously, in the empty hospital room of his mind, Alan reaches towards the foot of the bed, towards the Spaceman, towards the answer to the mysterious visitor's identity.

In the actual hospital room, the unconscious Alan lifts his arm and reaches towards the foot of the bed as the chaos continues around him. There is no one there. Millie sees this and jumps.

"What's he doing?" Max asks the doctor. Barratt barely looks up.

"Most likely he's hallucinating, due to the pressure on his brain." He turns to the nurse. "We've got to get him into surgery, STAT." She reaches for the phone.

Out on the front lawn, the Spaceman slowly turns towards Alan. The nighttime sky reflects off the tinted visor of his helmet. Alan can't make out the face inside. He sees his own reflection staring back at him.

The staff wheels Alan into the operating room to prep him for surgery. Max and Millie watch helpless from the window, clutching each other for support.

On the lawn, the Spaceman reaches up towards his helmet. There is a puff of depressurization as the helmet lifts off his head. At first this perplexes Alan. The face he sees hasn't changed, but he is no longer looking at a reflection. Alan is face to face with himself.

He blinks, and he is standing in the empty operating room, wearing the red spacesuit. He stares at himself lying on the operating table, only the self he sees is an old man, almost unrecognizable.

Out on the front lawn, Alan the Spaceman looks into the face of Alan the old man (or is it Alan's father?). Whoever he is, the man's eyes glisten, either with tears or from old age. Alan the Spaceman smiles.

In the empty operating room, the old man on the operating table has tears in his eyes. At the foot of the table, Alan the Spaceman smiles. The sounds of an actual, functioning operating room invade the scene.

"We're losing him!" the doctor yells, kicking activity into overdrive. Outside the operating room, Max and Millie watch helpless from the window as hospital staff surround and engulf Alan's body. A single, piercing note cuts the chaos.

Alan flatlines.

Millie buries her head into Max.

Out on the lawn, Alan the Spaceman is gone. The old man sways, as if asleep on his feet. A tear leaks from the corner of his eye as a shooting star cuts across the sky.

In the operating room of Alan's mind, the Spaceman has gone as well. The old man on the operating table breathes his last breath to the sound of the flatline.

Millie cries as the medical team attempts to revive Alan. Max puts an arm around her.

Alan the Spaceman steps out of the shadows in his mother's room at the nursing home. She sits propped up in bed, despite the late hour. Paul Langley sits opposite her, dressed in his black burial suit, bare feet resting lightly against the floor.

"Max?" Florence Langley calls out to the darkness. "Is that you?"

"No, Ma, it's me, Alan," he says. His mother bristles.

"I was expecting your brother. Take those shoes off."

Alan looks down at his moon boots, looks to his father. Paul Langley shrugs.

"It's up to you, boy. Whether you plan on staying or not."

Florence turns her head to reprimand her husband.

"You stay out of this, Paul. This whole situation's your fault to begin with."

"Is that a fact?" Paul draws the sentence out with comic incredulity. His amusement is lost on his ex-wife.

"And didn't I tell you to stop showing up unannounced?"

"Not here for you. Here for the boy." Paul nods towards his son. Alan looks from his father to his mother. It is her turn to get sarcastic.

"Well that's a first. Paul Langley, being there for his family."

Paul frowns at his ex wife, turns to Alan.

"Never mind her. You got something you need to say?"

Alan the Spaceman looks back and forth between his parents. Opens his mouth to speak, and—

The sound of the flatline intensifies, covering Alan's dialogue. His body loses substance, becoming opaque. His parents continue to watch as his very being breaks down, atom by atom, until they are staring at the empty space where their child once stood.

"He belongs to the stars now," Florence Langley says.

THE PARADOX TWINS
by ALBERT LANGLEY

You're reading my memoir, so I suppose it's obvious I didn't die in that hospital bed. It was touch and go there for a while, but I didn't even technically flatline. Flatlining, as depicted on TV, with the straight line and beeping monitor, is a myth. If you showed an audience how it happened in everyday life, they wouldn't realize the patient had died unless they'd had some medical training. *Asystole*, as flatlining is known in the medical profession, refers to a total lack of electrical activity in the heart. This activity generally doesn't stop dead. It gets weaker in increments, fluttering in and out of peaks and valleys, until a tiny wavy line peters across the bottom of the screen.

In my case, my blood pressure and heart rate dropped, which is cause for concern, but they never dipped so low that defibrillation became necessary. Seems I've developed a slower-than-average heart rate in my old age. Would have been nice if my GP had said something. Other than that, I don't know exactly what happened, as I slept through the whole ordeal, none the wiser until the doctors filled me in.

I'm sure Max's book turns the episode into an emotionally manipulative cliffhanger and milks it for all it's worth. When his publisher heard I was writing a book of my own, they rushed *Breakfast with the Monolith* into print to prevent me from spoiling whatever narrative surprises Max had in store. They even offered to put me up in a fancy, out-of-country hotel in an effort to keep my real-life survival a secret. Later I found out Max had wanted to kill my character off, but the publisher decided it would be less confusing for the reader if he hewed closer to the facts.

It's funny how the publisher decided on which facts were important to them and which ones weren't. Especially since I don't think they mattered to Max at all. To him, nothing was off limits. His choices were dictated by whatever he felt served the story best. It's one of his better qualities as a writer. It's also one of the things that makes him a shitty brother. Can you be a good memoirist without alienating friends and family? My money's on "no."[74]

Despite all this we've kept in better contact since the hotel room incident. The whole thing served to further reinforce the randomness of the universe, the most random event for me being Max not abandoning me in my time of need. I don't ever want the opportunity to return the favor, although I'd do it in a (bradycardic) heartbeat.

If our father was alive, or living on in some unexpected afterlife, or even floating around as star stuff, I'm sure he'd take credit for this lesson. It was one he espoused his whole life as a scientist, and one he used as an excuse for his flaws as a husband and a father. Whatever form he's taken, I'm sure he would be pleased. Or pissed, because hell, nothing ever pleased him.

---

[74] Fortunate, then, I have no living family. The Langleys are the only family I need.

Oh, and speaking of hell, our mother still insists he's burning there. Never change, Mom. Never change. Pretty soon you'll be the mother of *two* authors instead of one. Two and a half, if you can find it in your heart to consider your husband's bastard progeny part of the family. Take one for the team, Mom. I hear the nursing home needs a new sun room...

As for Millie, I haven't seen her since the hospital. She made the wise decision to distance herself from the Langley brothers after that, even though we're now officially half-siblings. Mrs. Blackford tells me Millie's working on a book of her own. A memoir. It's about—you guessed it—the whole sordid Langley affair. I wish her all the luck in the world, but I don't think I'll be reading it. I'm not looking forward to all the roundtable interview requests and reunion specials I'll be pitched once all three books see print. If you're reading this and have already seen me on one or seven, I assure you, desperation motivated my decision. If that out-of-country hotel offer from my brother's publisher still stands I could get the hell out of Dodge and take [REDACTED][75] on a nice trip.

Yeah, I met someone. Don't want to print her name because, you know, early days and all. Plus: privacy. After this book, I never want to air my personal business out in public again. Dirty laundry is one thing. Sure, it's embarrassing, but soiled clothes can be discarded.

---

[75] DOXXED: Mary Stafford, 42, full-time CPA, originally from Atlanta, GA.

Clean laundry, on the other hand. Clean laundry's worth keeping clean.

I met her at one of my brother's events. I know that sounds weird, but it's not what you think. Max had her ejected from the store in a literary rage because she continued to browse the aisles during his reading. I guess it reminded him too much of the early days. If only Mom had been there his embarrassment would have been complete. I went outside to apologize to the woman and we clicked. I have NOT brought her to visit my mother.

Max and I look more like twins these days. At least we did, until he grew that "authorly" beard of his. Maybe it's for the best. If we're both going to be out on the book tour circuit, we don't want people confusing us for one another. I credit diet and exercise for my transformation. Max maintains it's because I've boarded my own little rocket ship and accelerated out of my boring inertial frame, following a path contrail-blazed by him. He says I still have a long way to go, and won't actually catch up to him unless he slows down, which he doesn't plan on doing. I told him it's more likely he'll miscalculate his course and fly straight into a collapsing star. We both had a good laugh at that.

So what comes next? I don't think I'll be returning to the classroom any time soon. At least not as an instructor. I'd have to go into teacher witness protection and move to another town, where no one knew my true identity. Wouldn't mind scoring myself one of those honorary degrees from a prestigious university, though, if only to rub it in Max's face.

Not sure if I have another book in me after this one. I never planned on being a writer, it kind of fell into my lap. [REDACTED] has turned me on to poetry, and even though there's less of a chance of making a living writing verse, I'd like to try my hand at it. I've been reading a lot of science-based poetry these days. They say Oppenheimer, that destroyer of worlds, fancied himself an amateur poet. According to apocrypha he was the one on the receiving end of physicist Paul Dirac's famous quote, "The aim of science is to make difficult things understandable in a simpler way; the aim of poetry is to state simple things in an incomprehensible way. Thus, the two are incompatible."

As good a physicist as he was, I'm going to have to disagree with Dirac here. Science itself is inherently poetic, and it is possible to express this in poetic terms. As long as we don't go replacing actual scientific metrics with poetic meter, I'm sure the scientific community will survive.

I've yet to compose anything worth sharing, so I'll leave you with this: the first stanza of a poem my mother used to read to Max and I as children. "The Twins" by Henry Sambrooke Leigh. I never identified with the narrator of the poem as a child, as I was in denial of the similarities between my brother and I. But now that we're older, I can see the humor in it, especially as I've come to accept how alike we are. If it didn't describe us as children, it seems

to describe us as adults, or at least the slow change taking
place since we reunited at our father's funeral.

In form and feature, face and limb,
I grew so like my brother,
That folks got taking me for him,
And each for one another.
It puzzled all our kith and kin,
It reached a fearful pitch;
For one of us was born a twin,
Yet not a soul knew which.

THE THIRD TWIN
by MILLICENT BLACKFORD

This is a far cry from the speculative Young Adult novel I wanted to write, but it had to be done.[76] If I didn't get this out of my system it would have haunted me my entire (fingers crossed) career. Plus, as my agent would say, time may be money, but *timing* determines how much. Being rich has never been a priority for me, but I didn't flunk out of school and go through all that shit with Alan and Max to NOT take advantage of the situation. Must be the Langley in me.

But since I've gotten my personal life sorted, I've taken a much needed vacation from my newly discovered family. Relocating to Los Angeles has done wonders. Plus, my agent thinks she can get me some screenwriting work. Says they're looking for someone to do yet another pass on the *Breakfast with the Monolith* script, and it could use a woman's touch. If you ask me it needs more of a woman's kick to the face, and I'll probably pass, but there is another project I've had my eye on. I think I may have cracked the structural problems of bringing *Anthropica* to the big screen. Who knows, maybe they'll even let me direct. I've added Kathryn Bigelow and Patty Jenkins alongside Ursula K. Le Guin and Margaret Atwood in my hallowed pantheon of muses.

Speaking of agents, yes, Max helped. His agent even offered to take me on, but I figured putting a little buffer

---

[76] There are rumors the publisher hired a ghostwriter on *The Third Twin*, in an effort to churn the book out all the faster. Some claim that ghostwriter was Max, while just as many insist on Alan. Regardless, both camps cite similarities in voice and style as the smoking gun.

room between our careers would be prudent. So I decided on someone a little lower down the food chain. Someone hungry, who would make me their main focus. Max's agent put me in touch with an agent who put me in touch with Jess. She was a junior at the time, but ready to move up. Hopefully our careers will mature in tandem, barring any unforeseen shifts in the inertial frame.

Mom didn't want me to leave Boston, but she didn't put up a fight, either. She's hung up her boxing gloves. And yeah, I still call her Mom. I mean, the woman raised me. She earned it. And it's not like I can switch emotional gears like that. Besides, what the hell does she know about being an Aunt? Nothing, that's what. You can't teach an old dog new tricks, and I'm no dog trainer. Plus, I have no idea how to be a niece. That being said, I'm thinking about selling the house and bringing her out here. The sun would do her good. And I can't wait for her to meet Leone (no, not his real name).

Remember the quiet guy who sat in the back of my creative writing class? The one who could have easily been a footnote? Yep. Turns out he's doing okay for himself, as an assistant to some high profile studio exec. They call him *Leone* (as in *Sierra*, not *Sergio*), because when it comes to reading scripts, apparently he's got a knack for discovering gems, an instinct he cultivated during college.[77] In fact, he's got a certain crumpled up piece of paper smoothed out and framed, hanging in his office. He said it's a reminder to trust his instincts, and

[77] DOXXED: Leo Smith, age 30, originally from Boston, MA. NOT a Producer's Assistant. More like a glorified intern. Consider him a footnote. (This shit's too easy.)

that there's good work out there, no matter what everyone else says. I know it seems a little weird, and I'd be inclined to agree, if he wasn't so damned sincere.

That and he had no idea who I was at first. We'd crossed paths once or twice, but he didn't make the connection until he'd read one of my scripts. A story about two sisters engaged in a series of contests, judged by their mother and father. The whole thing takes place on the world stage in the form of a very popular YouTube channel run by the parents. Each week the siblings are assigned a challenge rooted in a different discipline. The winner of each week's challenge is awarded basic privileges while the loser is denied. Things like hot food, water, a bed to sleep in. Sound familiar? But wait, there's more.

As the punishments become more outlandish and inhumane, people assume the show is a hoax, scripted and shot in a studio, but no one can prove it. They just tune in every week to satisfy their curiosity. A sort of farcical commentary on fame in the internet generation, but also—you guessed it—an examination of sibling rivalry.

The studio hated it, but they're interested in *The Third Twin*, so maybe we can work something out. Leone wants to step up and produce, and the studio owes him for securing the rights to some weird barbarian comic a friend of his created.[78]

---

[78] Good old Howard! I can't believe Millie hasn't put two and two together. Frankly, there's quite a bit she hasn't put together.

BREAKFAST WITH THE MONOLITH – M. BLACKFORD[79] – 1/5/16 DRAFT

INT. FUNERAL HOME – DAY

A wake is in progress. Flowers, music, mourners. An OLD MAN lies in the coffin.

EXT. CEMETERY – DAY

Mourners and the Minister look on as a machine lowers the coffin into the ground. A FIT MAN (50s) stands in front. Could it be Max Langley?

INT. PAPER & GLUE – NIGHT

The Fit Man sits at a table piled high with books. A long line of people waits as he signs.

He returns a book with a smile. A BOOKSELLER ushers up the next in line. A WOMAN (late 20s) places her book on the table.

---

[79] Looks like Millie's agent knows how to make things happen.

For reference, these scenes followed the "Stargate Sequence" in most drafts of the *BwtM* script. The emotionally manipulative reversal Alan talked about.

The cover depicts the Langley twins as toddlers. One plays with a toy rocket, which obscures the face of the other.

The title reads: "THE PARADOX TWINS" by Albert Langley

                    FIT MAN
          And who should I make this out to?

                    WOMAN
          Well, if you're going by Albert
          now, I guess you'd better make it
          out to Millicent.

The Fit Man/Alan looks up to see Millie Blackford. Millie smiles.

INT. PUB - NIGHT

Alan and Millie sit across from each other in the same old booth.

                    MILLIE
          So this is where the famous
          Albert Langley wrote his first
          book.

                    ALAN
          Actually, I wrote most of it in the
          hospital, while Max was sick.

                    MILLIE
          That must have been hard.

                    ALAN
          It was. Max was constantly giving
          me notes.

Millie laughs.

                    ALAN (CONT'D)
          It was tough. The disease did a
          number on him. He wasn't the
          Max you remember.

                    MILLIE
          I wish I could have been there to
          say goodbye.

                    ALAN
          I know you do. But if anyone
          understood the obligation of
          career, it was Max.

                    MILLIE
          Still…

                    ALAN
          What about you? I hear you have a
          book of your own coming out.

                    MILLIE
          I do.

                    ALAN
          I'd love to read it.

                    MILLIE
          I just so happen to have an copy
          right here.

She hands Alan her book, "THE THIRD
TWIN."

He opens it. The dedication reads:
"FOR MY BROTHERS."

                    ALAN
          How long are you in town for?

                    MILLIE
          A couple more days.

           ALAN

Have time to come visit the wife
and kids tomorrow?

           MILLIE

Of course.

           ALAN

It's funny. Now that the book's
out and Max is gone, the publishers are talking about sending
me on tour. This is what I've
always wanted, but now that I have
it, I don't want to leave home.

           MILLIE

Time to climb up into that big,
phallic rocket ship.

They laugh.

         MILLIE (CONT'D)

Don't forget, if you take Special
Relativity out of the equation, it's
all about frame of reference.

           ALAN

I remember when you used to think
science was boring.

                    MILLIE
          That was before I knew I came
          from a family of scientists.

They lapse into silence.

                    MILLIE
          Do you still see him?

                    ALAN
          Who?

                    MILLIE
          Dad.

                    ALAN
          No, not since my coma.

                    MILLIE
          Did he ever say anything to you?

                    ALAN
          That last time together, we had a
          whole conversation.

                    MILLIE
          What did you guys talk about?

                    ALAN
That's the thing. I don't remember.

                    MILLIE
No?

                    ALAN
It was one of those weird dream
things. I remember feeling such
contentment, like I finally got to
connect with the man, but when I
woke up... the words were gone.

                    MILLIE
That's frustrating.

                    ALAN
What can you do? It was a coma
induced fantasy.

                    MILLIE
I don't know. I like to think
he's out there somewhere,
watching over us.

> ALAN
> Are you sure you're his daughter?
> Because you know how he felt
> about the afterlife.

> MILLIE
> Doesn't mean he was right.

EXT. ALAN'S HOUSE - NIGHT

Alan pulls into the driveway.

INT. ALAN'S HOUSE - NIGHT

Alan looks down at his TWIN SONS,
sleeping in their crib. His WIFE
joins him, plants a kiss on his
cheek.

INT. MILLIE'S HOTEL ROOM - NIGHT

Millie comes out of the bathroom,
gets into bed. She opens the same,
old paperback copy of "2001." She
nods off as she reads.

A figure in what appears to be a
spacesuit slowly becomes visible at
the foot of the bed.[80]

THE END

---

[80] She Hollywooded up the ending, but I think Millie did a fantastic job here. I doubt killing off Max's character made him happy, which I'm sure gave Alan and Millie great pleasure.

Speaking of which (and I saved this question for last, so as not to spoil the reader's vision), but who do we see playing the three leads? Obviously an unknown *ingenue* for Millie. A successor to the Jennifer Lawrence throne. That's what I would do if I were given the chance to produce. But what about the titular twins? Do you cast two different actors with similar faces and different body types? Non-identical brothers? Or do you let one actor tackle both roles with the help of makeup and wardrobe? A meaty gig for any actor to sink their teeth into, whether you go seasoned character actor or tentpole headliner.

THE LANGLEY SAGA
WILL CONTINUE...

...but not here, at unravelingtheparadox.com. As my subjects have moved on with their lives, so must I move on with mine. Because to me, this version of the story constitutes a completed work—with a beginning, middle, and end—and I would not be tethered to it indefinitely. Other projects require my attention. As a fan I will continue to follow the careers of Max, Millie, and Alan,[81] and may even post occasional news updates, but I no longer consider myself their unofficial chronicler and neither should you. I relinquish creative control. Their story belongs to the future artists of the world.

My reasons remain my own, and have nothing to do with my psychiatrist, who has encouraged me multiple times to step away and dismantle this website (as if you could UN-paint a picture, or UN-sing a song). She insists I have done nothing more than transfer my obsession from one object (myself) to another (the Langleys. Specifically, Millie). What is more, she claims I tend to blur the lines between fact and fiction, fantasy and reality, which at the least indicates sociopathic tendencies. (Again, she is not a writer, so please forgive her ignorance when it comes to matters creative.) Although she seems unconcerned with my many, *many* copyright infringements, she finds certain (innocuous) elements of my writing

---

[81] *Maximillialan* for all you shippers out there.

troubling, and while they are not enough for her to break confidentiality and alert the authorities, she has not ruled it out should new information come to light.[82]

But fear not, artists and readers. She does not have access to my real name or address. Which puts her at a disadvantage, as she knows I have hers.[83] And if she truly understands me as well as she thinks she does, as her condescending monotone indicates, she will know I am above all a cautious man. This website will live on. And I hope the people who discover the Langleys through this amalgam of CSS and HTML go on to follow their own path, and write their own version of this story, or their own story, or any story. That carries more importance for me than anything else, even outsider perceptions of my so-called mental fortitude. I began my introduction with a quote: *There are three sides to every story*. Obviously the Langley saga has grown to include more, but I do not consider my psychiatrist's one of them. Not as far as this website is concerned. Her insights exist only in her personal frame of reference. It's probably time to put an end to our relationship, anyway. Make a clean break, and start a new chapter in my life. I look forward to what the future holds.

T-minus ten...

The Webmaster
Joshua Chaplinsky (still a pseudonym)
2020

---

[82] Let her! *Everything is right on the page*, available for all to see! I have nothing to hide.

[83] At least she does now. Right, Margaret?

June 20th, 2020   **via email (street address unknown)**

Mr. Joshua Chaplinsky
Webmaster
www.unravelingtheparadox.com

Re: Use of copyrighted materials

Dear Mr. Chaplinsky,

THIS IS YOUR FINAL WARNING.

This law firm represents MASSPUB BOOKS and its subsidiary imprint NEXTDOOR PRESS. If you are represented by legal counsel, please direct this letter to your attorney and have them notify us of such representation.

We are writing to inform you that your continued unlawful usage of elements of THE THIRD TWIN by Millicent Blackford infringes upon our client's exclusive copyrights. Accordingly, you are hereby directed to immediately CEASE AND DESIST ALL COPYRIGHT INFRINGEMENT.

These usages include, but are not limited to, electronic dissemination of copyrighted material, as well as unlawful derivation of said material.

---

[84] Ha! These fools again. There's no narrative element here, but I found it fitting to end with the latest corporate attempt at stifling my art. It's not worth reading past the first paragraph (which, after the initial notice, I stopped doing). Just a regurgitated jumble of legalese and doublespeak about vague, nebulous laws no one really understands. I cut and pasted the whole thing to rub it in their faces. Because you can't control ideas. Remember, the artist is the true Maker of Rules.

Such derivation is considered a dilution of the owner's copyright and potentially damaging to their brand and revenue.

The owner of the original copyright also contests that the derivative work can be viewed as libelous, as it is based on a story of an autobiographical nature and purports, itself, to be "true." As MILLICENT BLACKFORD, the author of said copyrighted material, currently holds a civil harassment order against your person in the state of California (C.C.P. 527.6), the insertion of yourself (or any number of thinly veiled avatars) into the work on a public platform could be construed as a willful violation of that order, as well as a purposeful infliction of distress. This includes, but is not limited to, the following pseudonyms: JOSHUA CHAPLINSKY, JAGER CARTWRIGHT, PAUL LANGEVIN and LEO SMITH.

Under United States copyright law, MASSPUB BOOKS's copyrights have been in effect since the date that THE THIRD TWIN by Millicent Blackford was created. All copyrightable aspects of THE THIRD TWIN by Millicent Blackford are copyrighted under United States copyright law.

We have copies of your unlawful copies to preserve as evidence. Your actions constitute copyright infringement in violation of United States copyright laws. Under 17 U.S.C. 504, the consequences of copyright infringement include statutory damages of between $750 and $30,000 per work, at the discretion of the court, and damages of up to $150,000 per work for willful infringement. If you continue to engage in copyright infringement after receiving this letter, your actions will be evidence of "willful infringement."

We demand that you immediately (A) cease and desist your unlawful copying of THE THIRD TWIN by Millicent Blackford and (B) provide us with prompt written assurance within ten (10) days that you will cease and desist from further infringement of MASSPUB BOOKS's copyrighted works. If you do not comply with this cease and desist demand within this time period, MASSPUB BOOKS is entitled to use your failure to comply as evidence of "willful infringement" and seek monetary damages and equitable relief for your copyright infringement. In the event you fail to meet this demand, please be advised that MASSPUB BOOKS has asked us to communicate to you that it will contemplate pursuing all available legal remedies, including seeking monetary damages, injunctive relief, and an order that you pay court costs and attorney's fees. Your liability and exposure under such legal action could be considerable.

In addition, MILLICENT BLACKFORD will be pursuing charges against you in conjunction with the existing civil harassment order you are named in.[85]

Before taking these steps, however, my client wished to give you one final opportunity to discontinue your illegal conduct by complying with this demand within ten (10) days. Accordingly, please sign and return the attached *Agreement* within ten (10) days to

[FIRM NAME REDACTED]
[FIRM ADDRESS REDACTED]

If you or your attorney have any questions, please contact me directly.

Sincerely,

[REDACTED]

---

[85] Oh, Millie. I thought we talked about this? You can't charge what you can't find. Might as well issue an arrest warrant for a ghost. Looks like the Spaceman is going to have to pay you another visit...

ABOUT THE AUTHOR:

Joshua Chaplinsky is a pseudonym for the Webmaster of unravelingtheparadox.com. He is a college dropout who self-identifies as an artist—as opposed to an author—that paints with the words of others. His name appears at the bottom of every page of this website, each one representing a signature on a canvas. This is his first large scale work of collage. He currently rewrites history and pushes the boundaries of art from behind a computer screen on the American West Coast, hiding in plain sight of the corporate Hollywood elite.

A PARADOX UNRAVELED

At this point I'm assuming you've already finished the book. It's called an afterward for a reason. Still, just to be safe...

BEWARE OF SPOILERS!

Okay, with that out of the way—where to begin? Yeah, yeah, I know... "time is a construct," but we should probably begin at the beginning, regardless. If that doesn't suit you, isn't weird enough after what you've read, I suggest starting from the end and reading every other paragraph until you reach the top, then turning around and doing the same in the opposite direction. Continue reading every other remaining, *unread* paragraph until you return to the end. This pattern should result in a continuous elimination of content, a consistent halving of words. Repeat until you've read the entire afterward and/or are thoroughly confused. If anyone discovers any hidden meaning this way, I'd love to hear it.

Moving on.

It took over a decade to produce the slim volume you currently hold in your hands. That's conception to birth, although there was plenty of down time. A few... what you might refer to as *miscarriages* or *terminations*, if we're sticking with this art-as-child metaphor. Either way, isn't my baby cute? Lord knows enough people expected them to be developmentally disabled, which... let's be honest, after reading the thing, chances are they still will.

Anyway...

The Paradox Twins went through numerous changes during its ten year gestation period. It started out as a film script, my seventh, and was supposed to be my attempt at writing something accessible. My entry ticket into the Hollywood funfair, if you will (although you probably shouldn't). Up until that point I had toiled under the impression that screenwriting was where narrative art went to flourish. Ah, to be young again...

My earliest notes date back to December 2010, when the project was still called *Breakfast with the Monolith*, based on an image from the end of Kubrick's *2001: A Space Odyssey*, of an aged David Bowman taking a quiet meal in the white room. Although the monolith does appear in said room, this doesn't occur while Bowman eats, but I liked the idea of someone sitting down to table with a large, emotionless slab as if it were a real person.

Sound accessible enough? This not being a load-bearing narrative idea, I knew I needed more. I don't remember exactly when I discovered the thought experiment known as the Twins Paradox—thanks to David Lynch I'd long been fascinated by doubles and doppelgangers—but I immediately saw the thematic potential once I did.

The notes in question took the form of a one page outline, sketching out various early turning points in a three act story. (See? Accessible!). One thing in particular that stands out: Millie sleeping with both brothers, an idea which, thankfully, I jettisoned during my first draft. But even by the polished, final draft of the script (dated 2/9/14), Millie existed mostly as a foil for the Langley brothers, and while she had an arc of her own, and the script somehow managed to pass the Bechdel test—most likely on a technicality, or, as I like to call it, a *Bechd*nicality—she was not on equal footing as "a third twin." Her final form in the novel is much more nuanced, and her evolution as a character is something I am quite proud of. At the very least I look at it as a bullet dodged.

That being said, was the finished product the highly marketable one I had envisioned? Eh… I'd certainly written *less* marketable scripts. Beta-readers said the story contained too much incest for a mainstream movie. I countered that there wasn't *any* actual incest, which was more than I could say for both *The Empire Strikes Back* and *Back to the Future*, and those were considered family films.

The incest stays in the picture!

Not that it mattered. It wasn't long after that 2/9/14 draft of *The Paradox Twins* that I fell out of love with screenwriting and shifted my focus to short fiction. I had decided I wanted to actually *sell* what I wrote, no matter how miniscule the payment, and wanted people to actually read it, no matter how small the group. So into a drawer the script went, along with its predecessors and all my Hollywood dreams. At this point I was burnt out on longform storytelling, and had no interest in novel writing whatsoever. Like your chunky cousin who drives a UPS truck year round, I was officially a shorts man.

I began writing and submitting, landing myself an acceptance here and there. In November 2015, my short story "Letters to the Purple Satin Killer" was published in Thuglit #20. (It was later reprinted at Trigger Warning Short Fiction and in my collection, *Whispers in the Ear of A Dreaming Ape*.) Shortly thereafter, I was informed that a respected editor expressed a fondness for the story, and it might not be the worst idea for me to reach out to them. The resulting exchange culminated in an invitation—to submit a novel, if ever I decided to write one. I filed this flattering offer away for posterity, because as you will recall, I had no interest in writing a novel at the time. None whatsoever.

Fast forward to September 2016. I was invited to hang out with Christoph Paul and Leza Cantoral of CLASH Books at the Brooklyn Book Festival. They allowed me a portion of their space to display my novel-in-name-but-not-in-length, *Kanye West—Reanimator* (which is a whole other origin story). We chatted about writing and publishing throughout the day, and eventually the conversation turned towards current projects. Christoph expressed interest in publishing me, and in the heat of the moment I told him about a script I had written called *The Paradox Twins*, which I was toying with turning into a novel (which, at the time, I swear I wasn't).

What prompted me to say this? Maybe my whole disinterest-in-writing-a-novel schtick was a form of insecurity—garden variety fear of rejection. Maybe I *wanted* to write a novel, and all I needed was a little validation. In the back of my mind lurked the offer from that respected editor. When I had told them I didn't have a completed novel to pitch, they said all they needed was an outline and the first fifty pages to determine if it was something they wanted to represent. Fifty pages was nothing. My script already existed, all the heavy lifting had been done, why waste the work? All I had to do was flesh out the descriptions. It'd be easy: submit the excerpt, and if the editor was actually interested, if I received a concrete commitment from them, *then* I would finish the book. Those were the only circumstances under which I'd even consider writing a novel.

But then I thought, wait a minute... if I was going to write a novel, did I *really* want it to be a straightforward adaptation of this (admittedly not-very-commercial) script? I had been experimenting with form in my short fiction, and so many of my favorite novels—the ones that excited me the most—took creative risks. If I was going to put in the effort, shouldn't I go all out? Write the type of story I would want to read? (Also, this thought was not unconnected to the problem of what POV to tell the story from.) So I decided on using multiple, conflicting viewpoints in the form of overlapping book excerpts. It made the project more interesting, and the narrative kind of lent itself to that approach, anyway.

With that problem solved, I began writing in earnest. Pretty soon I was closing in on a solid fifty pages. But then I had another pesky thought—what if the narrative was *still* too straightforward for my self-imposed expectations? (Also, I needed to solve the problem of why this hodgepodge of excerpts would exist in the first place.) What if—and hear me out—I added a *fourth* POV, in the form of a series of footnotes, that gave a legitimate reason for the structure, and cast a new light on the story as a whole? BOOSH! That was the precise moment I fell in love with the idea of *The Paradox Twins* as a novel.

That was also the precise moment a new doubt reared its head. Could *The Paradox Twins* actually *be* a novel? At the rate I was going, I estimated my 100 page script would translate to roughly 50,000 words of prose, exceeding the accepted 40k maximum for a novella, but falling short of the 65 to 75k industry minimum for a novel.

But then I thought of all the short "novels" that were technically novellas. Some even falling in the same "no man's land" as mine, such as *The Great Gatsby*, *The Crying of Lot 49*, *True Grit*, and *War of the Worlds*. If editors and publishers wanted to quibble over how to classify my book, so be it. I wasn't going to let some arbitrary number dictate the length of my story. It would be the length it needed to be, as David Lynch would say (even though I complained about the length of the film he said this about). Plus, the formatting of the screenplay sections would pad out the page count. *The Paradox Twins* would at least have the girth of a novel!

The integration of the footnotes into the narrative took some tinkering. Inspired by Barthelme, I started looking at my novel as a collage, incorporating not only multiple memoir excerpts, but documents of public record and other ephemera. This was the final piece of the puzzle, for me. By June 2017, I had a presentable fifty pages, which I shot off to the interested editor, fingers crossed. Within a week I received a reply:

"While I applaud the innovativeness of the novel, I found it a bit too challenging for most readers. Your short description of the novel seemed appealing, but I was not captured by the actual pages. Too many interruptions in the narrative, and an opening section that will prompt editors to delete the submission."

Can't say I wasn't surprised. It was almost a relief. Still, I kept writing. It's like the editor's criticism was an encouragement. And now that I had a better idea of what the project was, a list of potential publishers formulated in my mind. Speaking of which...

A few months later, Brooklyn Book Fest rolled back around. Once again I hung out with Christoph and Leza, and once again the subject of current projects was broached. I told them I had committed to writing *The Paradox Twins*. They told me they were interested. They asked if I had any publishers in mind... and I told them that [redacted mid-size indie publisher] was my ideal home for it. In retrospect, this seems counter-intuitive (i.e.: dumb as hell). To their credit, they were totally gracious about what some might have viewed as a slight, telling me to keep them posted instead of telling me to fuck off.

By February 2018 I had a completed draft. I submitted it to the [redacted mid-size indie] and settled in to wait. According to their website, their turnaround was six months. In the back of my mind I thought, be patient. In six months you'll get a rejection, you can say you tried, and then you can submit to CLASH.

Six nail-biting months went by. I followed up with [redacted mid-size indie]. They responded almost immediately, saying they were pretty far behind, but were looking forward to checking *Twins* out. They had also updated the response time listed on their website to twelve months. I pondered what this meant for me and my submission. Could I wait that long? What if it took longer? According to Duotrope, [redacted mid-size indie] had a submission that had been pending for a whopping 563 days! And there were plenty other submissions in the slush on top of that.

What was I to do? Alienate CLASH and lose a great opportunity to wait another year (minimum) for what would most likely be a rejection? Was I being foolish? Impatient? And even if [redacted mid-size indie] did say yes, by the time the book actually came out, I would have spent years floundering in doubt without a new release.

So I hatched a cake-and-eat-it-too type plan. I followed up with CLASH, informing them of the latest development. Then I pitched them on a short story collection to bridge the gap. And you know what? They accepted! Suckers! (Just kidding.) So we got the ball rolling on *Whispers in the Ear of A Dreaming Ape*, and my appetite for progress was momentarily sated.

But the calm only lasted a few months. I couldn't get the math out of my head. I ran the stats over and over, the potential outcomes—especially the worst case scenarios—and finally decided it wasn't worth it. Why was I in denial? CLASH was the ideal publisher for *The Paradox Twins*, and they had been more than patient about my dalliance.

So in February 2019, I withdrew my submission from [redacted mid-size indie publisher] and informed CLASH I had sown my wild oats and was ready to settle down if they'd still have me. Thankfully, their answer was yes.

Whispers... was released in October of 2019. I joined Christoph and Leza at BBF once again to hawk early copies. I also participated in my first ever live reading, at Sisters in Brooklyn, as part of an all-CLASH lineup of authors. It was an amazing experience (you can find it on Youtube). I dressed like a priest and made the audience stand for the duration of my reading, *a la* the opening prayer at mass. Up on that stage, God visited a holy vision of future promotional performances upon me. The crowds… the adoration... the sales...

A few months later, reality came calling. COVID hit.

Faith shattered, my thoughts turned from religion to science, back to the subject of twins. CLASH only had one substantial editorial note on my novel manuscript—too many footnotes. (You thought it was gonna be about incest, didn't you?)

My original intent with the character behind the footnotes was for them to be a kind of obnoxious internet know-it-all, a self-proclaimed authority hiding behind their computer screen. It gave me an excuse to fill the manuscript with all sorts of bizarre factual tidbits and humorous asides. And while these things did establish said character as obnoxious, they didn't do much to further the narrative. Hell, most of them were barely thematically relevant, amounting to little more than unnecessary story interruptions (like that editor had said). So at CLASH's suggestion I cut more than half of them. Then, I went about sculpting what remained.

In the end, it was a great note, because I realized I needed the footnotes to function as part of the story, not just comment on it. The character needed to have a connection to Millie and the Langleys, be more than a passive observer. They needed to reveal things about themself when they discussed the lives of these people. I wanted the footnotes to have their own arc, build to their own climax, and affect the story as a whole, changing the way the reader looked at everything that came before. With CLASH's guidance I achieved that. At the least I came a lot closer to my goal than I otherwise would have.

POSSIBLE SPOILERS FOR A BOOK BESIDES MY OWN

Another big inspiration on the ending of *Twins* (which I didn't realize until *after* the fact) was *Diary* by Chuck Palahniuk. I'll try not to spoil Chuck's book completely, even though the ending plays a major part in this anecdote. I had received an ARC of *Diary* and was showing it off to a group of envious friends (this is waaaaay back in

2003). I was flipping through the back matter, something I enjoyed doing before embarking on a new read, and saw what looked to be a reproduction of a fan letter sent to Chuck. "Hey guys, listen to this…" I said to my friends. A chorus of protests erupted, hands clamped over ears. "This doesn't give anything away," I assured them and started to read. All it took was one sentence for me to realize I'd spoiled *Diary*'s big twist. My friends were *not* happy. It took a long time to live that one down, and it stuck with me. When I was searching for exactly how to intertwine the various threads of my novel, that experience provided the template.

That pretty much brings us up to the present. Now that I've written one novel, does that make me a novelist? Will I attempt to do it all again? I'm currently working on adapting another old screenplay. I doubt I'll do this for every script I ever wrote, but there are certain stories I want to see the light of day. And there's something about the adaptation process that appeals to me. More so than writing a novel from scratch. The screenplay functions as a detailed outline, providing only the most necessary information. From there I embellish where appropriate. I suppose this process contributes to a more minimal, cinematic style.

It's also allowed me the freedom to experiment with structure and form. Having the whole story laid out in front of me, it's easier to deconstruct without losing sight of the whole. And since I've already written the "accessible" version of the story, I'm not precious about the details. It's more interesting for me to do something different with the material.

As for screenwriting, I'm not that interested in Hollywood anymore. Sure, if someone offered me a million dollars to write an arachno-human movie, I'd do it, but I don't think scripts are the right vehicle for the stories I want to tell. That said, I would find it ironic if a book I wrote based on an old screenplay was optioned for film and turned back into a screenplay and then a movie. Talk about taking the scenic route.

The road I'm *currently* on has been a long one, but that's allowed me to refine my vision, tweak the details, and (I hope) get everything right. When will you see another book from me? I'm not sure. The old adage about having your entire life to write your first novel and a mere year to write your second lives in the back of my mind. I guess the Lynchian answer would be, it'll be done when it feels done, like the first one.

Until then, I hope you've enjoyed the journey as much as I have.

Joshua Chaplinsky (not a pseudonym)
January 2021

Joshua Chaplinsky is the author of *Kanye West—Reanimator* and the story collection *Whispers in the Ear of A Dreaming Ape*. He is the Managing Editor of *LitReactor.com*. His short fiction has been published by *Vice, Vol. 1 Brooklyn, Thuglit, Severed Press, Perpetual Motion Machine Publishing*, and *Broken River Book*s. Follow him on Twitter at @jaceycockrobin. More info at joshuachaplinsky.com.

CPSIA information can be obtained
at www.ICGtesting.com
Printed in the USA
BVHW072259150421
605033BV00003B/134